WHEN CAPTAIN KATHRYN JANEWAY MATERIALIZED IN THE TRANSPORTER ROOM OF THE *U.S.S. ENTERPRISE* . . .

she was pleased and flattered but not altogether surprised to see that none other than Captain Jean-Luc Picard was present to greet her.

"Permission to come aboard," she said lightly.

"Very happily granted," he replied, stepping forward with his hand outstretched. Janeway grasped it and swiftly covered it with her other hand.

"Kathryn," he said heartily, his hazel eyes warm with affection. "My God, it's good to see you. I could scarcely believe it when I saw *Voyager* soaring toward us out of that cloud of debris," he said. "We had been ready to fight the Borg, not welcome home a lost traveler."

"What can I say?" she quipped. "I like to make an entrance . . ."

D0311102

STAR TREK VOYAGER®

HOMECOMING

CHRISTIE GOLDEN

Based upon STAR TREK®
created by Gene Roddenberry
and STAR TREK: VOYAGER
created by Rick Berman & Michael Piller
& Jeri Taylor

POCKET BOOKS

New York   London   Toronto   Sydney   Singapore

An *Original* Publication of POCKET BOOKS

POCKET BOOKS, a division of Simon & Schuster, Inc.
1230 Avenue of the Americas, New York, NY 10020

STAR TREK is a Registered Trademark of Paramount Pictures.

This book is published by Pocket Books, a division of Simon & Schuster, Inc., under exclusive license from Paramount Pictures.

ISBN: 0-7434-6754-X

First Pocket Books printing June 2003

10   9   8   7   6   5   4   3   2

POCKET and colophon are registered trademarks of Simon & Schuster, Inc.

For information regarding special discounts for bulk purchases, please contact Simon & Schuster Special Sales at 1-800-456-6798 or business@simonandschuster.com

Printed in the U.S.A.

*This one is for the valiant crew
of the* U.S.S Voyager:

*Kate Mulgrew
Robert Beltran
Tim Russ
Robert Picardo
Robert Duncan McNeill
Roxann Dawson
Garrett Wang
Jeri Ryan
Ethan Phillips
and
Jennifer Lien*

Thanks for the adventure.

ACKNOWLEDGMENTS

Writing a book doesn't take place in a vacuum. I've had the assistance and support of many during this remarkable project. First and foremost, I'd like to thank my husband, Michael Georges, who's been willing to share his house with the crew of the *U.S.S. Voyager* for many a year now. He and my good friend Robert Amerman have often helped me brainstorm when I've reached a problem spot and I'm very grateful. Thanks also to a great group of friends and fellow authors— Mark Anthony, Chris Brown, Raven Amerman, Stan and Kathy Kirby, and Carla Montgomery. You guys are the best.

Supportive too have been my parents, James R. and Elizabeth C. Golden. They are sometimes a bit bemused by their wild child, but well do I remember the efforts made to get me home in time for *Star Trek* reruns. Looks like it all paid off.

Thanks also go to my agent, Lucienne Diver, who had no idea what she was starting almost ten years ago when she said casually, "Would you be interested in doing any books for Star Trek?" There was only one answer for that one.

A very special thank-you is due to John Ordover, for entrusting me with the care and feeding of the *Voyager* crew as we all head out together in this new direction. It's an honor to be the one selected to create the relaunch, and his support has been unwavering. Thank you, John.

Finally, a deep and heartfelt thank-you to all my fans. I never lose sight of the fact that my readers are the ones who make it possible for me to continue to write these wonderful stories. You have sent me hundreds of e-mails over the years, all of them expressing your appreciation for my work and anticipation of this project. It's taken a little longer than we all thought, but sometimes you have to take the time to do something right. And I really wanted to do this right! Let's hope you think I succeeded.

And so the voyage continues. . . .

> Thanks and blessings to you all from
> Denver, Colorado
> —Christie Golden

HOMECOMING

PROLOGUE

AGE THREE

She is alone, as she usually is, sitting in a corner far away from anyone's notice. Wetness soaks her bottom, but she says nothing. She is too fearful of the Hand. The Hand descended without any reason she could fathom, to strike hard against her small, soft cheeks, or seize her chubby arms, leaving bruises that would later disappear with the hum of something shiny and metallic. Young as she is, she already knows it is best to say nothing, to draw no attention to herself, to sit alone in the corner and play with the one small toy she is permitted to have.

Vaguely, she remembers a time before the man had come, when her mother's eyes shone and her lips parted in smiles and she laughed like the sun. When the girl was held close and kissed, and slept deeply, and dreamed dreams of moonbeams and ponies.

Now her mother is silent, sending that same message to her daughter. Her eyes are dull and she no longer laughs. Her mother, too, lives in fear of the Hand. And the girl's dreams now are of screams and blood.

She plays with Dolly, making the toy dance and sing as she, the flesh-and-blood girl, cannot.

A shadow falls over her. She freezes in terror.

The Hand reaches down, and she shrinks back. But the Hand has not come for her, but for Dolly. It grabs the old-fashioned toy. There is a bellow of something incoherent but very, very angry, and the Hand rips Dolly's head from her rag shoulders.

The girl whimpers, very softly. She cannot help herself. The Hand descends and she falls hard on the floor. She knows better than to rise or cry out, so she lies quietly, blood trickling from her mouth, her heart beating as fast as a rabbit's, until the shadow leaves.

The owner of the Hand has lurched off somewhere else. She hears the voice of her mother, high and strained and tight with fear, and turns away. The girl cannot let herself hear her mother's cries. If she does, she somehow knows, she will go mad.

For a moment, she simply stares at the mangled toy. Then, slowly, she picks up Dolly's torn body in one hand, her severed head in the other, and continues to play.

Chapter

1

TOM PARIS LOOKED AT THE NEWBORN, only a few minutes old, cradled awkwardly in his arms. She weighed only a few kilos, but felt so solid, so real to him. Her skin was reddish brown and wrinkled. Thick, coarse black hair covered her skull, which was larger even than a human baby's. With a tender finger, he traced the small ridges that furrowed her brow. As he watched, she yawned and waved a tiny fist in the air, almost defiantly, as if she dared anyone to come between her and a nap.

"She's the most beautiful thing I've ever seen," he said, and even as he acknowledged his daughter's wrinkled ugliness, he knew the words were completely true. He glanced over at B'Elanna. "Except, of course, for her mother."

3

Gently, he sat down on the sickbay bed beside her as she smiled tiredly at him.

"Nice save," she said, with a hint of her old robust demeanor.

"How's Mommy feeling?" he asked.

"Mommy's felt better," she admitted, and extended her arms for the child.

"Mother and child are just fine, though Mother is understandably cranky," said the Doctor. "You should be able to return to duty in approximately three days, Lieutenant. I feel compelled to inform you that I have downloaded everything in the database on the care of both Klingon and human infants." He preened a bit. "I'd make an excellent baby-sitter."

Tom grinned and gave his wife the baby, and his arms felt oddly empty as B'Elanna guided the child to her breast. He could get into this whole father thing, he thought.

"Janeway to Lieutenant Paris."

Tom grimaced, then replied, "Paris here."

"Report to my ready room."

He looked at B'Elanna. "Aye, Captain." Reluctantly he rose. "I thought we were on parental leave, but apparently duty calls. Sorry, girls."

B'Elanna gave him a strange look that he couldn't read. She reached out and touched his face tenderly. "I love you, Tom."

Now, why would she pick this time to say that? What was going on in that head of hers? "I love you too," he said, taking the hand that caressed his cheek and kissing it. "Both of you. Be back as soon as I can."

When he reached the bridge, he was surprised to see Captain Janeway sitting in her command chair, not in the ready room. He raised an eyebrow in question. In response, she nodded toward the room. "In the ready room, Mr. Paris."

This was getting downright confusing. "Yes, ma'am," he said.

The door hissed open. An imposing-looking, white-haired man rose from where he had been sitting at Janeway's desk. Tom's throat went dry.

"Dad," he breathed. Then, snapping to attention, he said, "Your pardon, sir. I mean, good day, Admiral Paris."

Of course, this was going to happen. Admiral Owen Paris had been heavily involved in Project *Voyager*. Tom knew that. Of course, as the project's nominal head, Paris would be the first to board when the lost vessel finally returned home. But Tom had been so thoroughly engrossed in thoughts of his wife and child that the likelihood that he would soon be reunited with his father had completely slipped his mind. Now he understood B'Elanna's peculiar look as he had left. She had figured it out before he had.

Admiral Paris's face was carefully neutral. *Damn,* thought Tom, *he looks so much older, so much more careworn.* The years that had passed since they last spoke had not been kind to him. Tom wondered how he appeared in his father's eyes.

Admiral Paris folded his hands behind his back, mirroring his son's formal stance.

"Lieutenant Paris. It's . . . it's good to see you. I'm glad you completed your mission so successfully. Your captain has many glowing things to say about you."

"No more than I have to say about her, sir. It's been a privilege to serve with her these past seven years." Why were his eyes stinging so? And that lump in his throat. . . .

Later, Tom would never be able to remember just which of them had made the first move. Maybe both of them did. But the next thing he knew, he was in his father's arms. It was a sensation he had not experienced since—he couldn't remember. Had his father ever embraced him so freely, so tightly, before? Had *he* ever wanted to open his arms to the rigid authority figure the untouchable, aloof Admiral Paris had always represented?

It didn't matter. His head resting on his father's shoulder, Tom smelled the familiar scent of aftershave, and for the first time really believed that, finally, he was going home.

"Dad," he whispered, brokenly.

"My boy," Owen Paris replied, his own voice hoarse. "My boy. I'm so glad you're home."

They sat and talked for a long, long time. Paris noted that they avoided anything of real import, like whether or not he'd be put back in jail or the fact that Admiral Paris was a grandfather. Tom was shocked to learn that, on a whim, his father had decided to take a cooking class and was laughing out loud at an anecdote about what "blackened chicken" *really* meant when the door hissed open.

Janeway stood there, smiling. "I wanted to give you

some time alone together before I called the senior staff for Admiral Paris's preliminary debriefing. Tom, does he know . . . ?" She lifted an eyebrow in question.

"Before we begin, Captain," said Tom, standing straight with pride, "is there time for my father to meet his daughter-in-law and granddaughter?"

Admiral Paris came as close to openmouthed gaping as Tom had ever seen in his life. Tension raced through him. Time to drop the other shoe: "B'Elanna will be so happy to see you, sir."

He knew Admiral Paris knew who B'Elanna Torres was. A half-Klingon and, like his son, a former Maquis. Silently, Tom pleaded that the fragile new camaraderie they had just established would weather this new storm.

There was a long, taut pause. Then a slow smile spread across the lined face. "It would be a pleasure."

When Tuvok reported to sickbay per the Doctor's orders, he felt a rush of surprise, which he quelled at once. Standing there calmly, his hands folded behind his back, was his eldest son, Sek.

"Greetings, Father," said Sek calmly. "It is good to see you."

"And you, my son. I assume that the Doctor requested your presence to administer the *fal-tor-voh?*"

Sek nodded. "Admiral Paris contacted me approximately fourteen hours ago. I studied the disease extensively during my trip to rendezvous with *Voyager.* I believe I am adequately prepared to meld with you, Father."

Privately, Tuvok wondered. A few hours spent reading material on such an intricate, complicated procedure hardly rendered his son, intelligent though he was, "adequately prepared." But he knew the situation was worsening. He looked at the Doctor, who answered Tuvok's wordless question.

"The genetic link is more important than actual familiarity with the procedure," the Doctor said. "And frankly, Commander, time is of the essence. I don't think anything would be served by waiting until Sek has learned more."

"Very well," said Tuvok. To Sek, he said, "We'll return to my quarters."

"If you don't mind," said the Doctor, "I'd rather have you here, so I can monitor your response. Not to insult you, Sek, but there's a chance that something might go wrong."

"It is impossible to insult me, Doctor," Sek replied. "I have no emotional response to critiques or commentary on my skills or lack thereof. Therefore, I can be neither flattered nor insulted."

"Vulcans," the Doctor muttered, rolling his eyes. Tuvok hesitated. This was an intimate, private ceremony. And yet, he was forced to admit that the Doctor had logic on his side. Reluctantly, he lay down on the biobed. He glanced over to see B'Elanna watching him; then she quickly looked away and returned her attention to nursing her child.

"I offer my congratulations on the healthy birth of your child," he said, somewhat stiffly.

"Thank you, Tuvok," she replied. She uttered no question or commentary on what she was witnessing, for which Tuvok was silently grateful. "Doctor," she said suddenly, "Tom and his father are coming down to meet me and Miral. I'd like to receive them in my quarters, if that's all right."

"As long as you go directly from that bed to your bed, you should be fine. The brief walk won't hurt you, and actually would be good for you. But if you start feeling weak, let me know at once, and don't overtire yourself."

"Believe me, I won't," said Torres. She eased out of bed, tapped her combadge, and, cradling the infant, headed out of sickbay while talking. "Tom, can you meet us in our quarters? I'm getting very tired of sickbay. . . ."

Tuvok gazed after her, grateful for her discretion. The Doctor brought a chair for Sek, then placed cortical monitors on both Vulcans' heads. Discreetly, he stepped as far away as possible.

Tuvok looked up at his son. To his consternation, he felt a rush of emotion. He had missed his family so much. Sek saw the reaction and recognized it for what it was: a sign that the disease was progressing.

"Do not worry, Father," he said gently. "Soon, these distractions will be gone." Sek closed his eyes, calming himself, then reached and placed his long, slim fingers on his father's brow. "My mind to your mind . . . your thoughts to my thoughts. . . ."

Sek's presence in his mind was like oil poured on churning water to Tuvok. At first, there was only a surface calm; then, gradually, Sek's thoughts penetrated deeper. He felt the young man's mind traversing his own, finding and searching out the synapses that carried the destructive virus.

He and his son had not melded since Sek was an infant. Tuvok, T'Pel, and Sek had bonded then in an extremely deep and profound union of minds. It was an ancient rite, lost for centuries and then rediscovered, that dated back to when Vulcans first began to harness the incredible powers of the mind. It had been easiest to meld with family members with whom one shared blood, then with more distant relatives, then strangers and, finally in recent history, members of other species. But the initial bonding, established so that the helpless infant could be linked to his parents more firmly, had been the most sacred and powerful.

It was this familiarity that swept through Tuvok now. The irony was not lost on him that this time, it was his son who was nurturing him, not the other way around. In this case, the bonding was to protect father, not child.

Sek's thoughts raced through Tuvok's mind, finding the damaged part of the older Vulcan's brain. There they were, the mutated cells, and Tuvok could see in his mind's eye that they were unnatural and out of harmony with the complex, delicate balance that was the Vulcan brain. The disease was spread through the neurological pathways. Tuvok knew that Sek, whose mind was undamaged, would be instructing his father's own cells to protect the uninfected part of the brain. The blood bond between them magnified the intimacy of the connection. It was the only way the condition could have been treated. Reaching so deeply would not have been possible without that link.

On a cellular level, Sek began to "speak" to Tuvok's brain. *There has been damage here. These cells are dangerous. You are not to access them any longer.* Gently, but firmly, Sek urged the cells to put up their own barriers. Information and stimuli were henceforth to bypass these areas. They were to become inert. Tuvok felt a strange rush, an imaginary tingling sensation as, under Sek's gentle urging, areas of his brain that had hitherto never been used opened up and responded to stimuli. Cell by cell, Sek isolated and rerouted the way Tuvok's brain would function. For several long minutes, Sek gently disentangled his own thoughts from Tuvok's.

Just before Sek withdrew, Tuvok felt a powerful, joyful wave wash through him. It was the love that his son felt for his father, the delight at being able to help him. Tuvok saw a small Vulcan child, and knew it to be his granddaughter T'meni, named for Tuvok's own mother. They would not speak of it, but here, in the most intimate joining that was possible for any two Vulcans, Tuvok acccpted that love and returned it as passionately.

Then his thoughts were his alone. He opened his eyes and gazed up into the impassive visage of Sek.

"How do you feel?" asked the Doctor.

Tuvok sat up, looked from his son to the Doctor, and announced, "I believe I am cured."

When the door hissed open, B'Elanna tried hard not to look as worried and apprehensive as she felt. Tom had told her only that he and Admiral Paris were coming down to meet her and Miral. He had told her nothing of how their own meeting went. She had guessed it had gone well, because of the lightness in her husband's voice, but that could have been an act for overhearing ears.

But when she saw Tom's nearly ear-to-ear grin—the grin she saw only when he was so happy he simply could not wipe it from his face, no matter how hard he tried to play cool and collected—she knew that her worries had been for nothing.

And when the imposing Admiral Owen Paris, practically a legend in his own time, reached toward her with outstretched hands, clasped her own, and kissed her warmly on the cheek, she almost wept.

"My son always had an eye for beauty," said Admiral Paris. "I'm pleased to see that he has learned to value character as well. I've read your captain's report on you, Lieu— B'Elanna. Both of you seem to have won her respect and affections."

"Thank you, Admiral," she said, her voice thick.

"You may call me Owen, if you like," he said. "Now, let me see this lovely little grandchild of mine."

Torres handed Miral over to her grandfather and reached for Tom's hand. The older man handled the tiny infant with surprising grace, smiling down into her little face with obvious pleasure.

"You handle babies quite well . . . Owen," said Torres, trying out the name with caution.

Admiral Paris smiled. "I've certainly spent enough time with them. You never knew, did you, Tom, that I was the one in charge of diaper changing?"

Judging by Tom's dumbfounded expression, he clearly did not. Torres smothered a smile at the thought of this distinguished elderly man changing Tom's soiled diapers, but the ease with which he carried Miral made his statement believable. He looked down at his new daughter-in-law and the smile faded somewhat.

"Tom and I discussed your family situation on our way here," he said. B'Elanna felt the heat of embarrassment rise in her cheeks. "I understand that you are without family."

"Not entirely correct," she said. "My father . . . chose not to be with me and my mother when I was young. I spoke to him for the first time in years just weeks ago. I have reason to believe that my mother died while we were in the Delta Quadrant."

"That was what Tom said," Admiral Paris confirmed. "I wanted to tell you that now you do have family. You and Miral are now dear and valued members of the Paris clan. My wife and I will love you like our own child." He turned to look at Tom and said, "And that is a great deal indeed."

Torres smiled, even though she felt like crying with joy. "Thank you, sir. That means a lot to us."

"Now, when *Voyager* first appeared," Admiral Paris continued, "we of course immediately notified all families. Nearly everyone has recorded messages from loved ones. Once I learned who my new daughter-in-law was, I checked to see if we had any for her. We did—two."

Torres's breath caught. She couldn't think of any one person who'd want to send her a message, let alone two. Admiral Paris handed them to her. "If you'd like to view them in private, Tom and I can—"

"No." B'Elanna spoke swiftly. "You are my family now. Whatever this is, whoever sent it, you can watch it with me."

After a moment Tom nodded and activated the view-screen.

A handsome man with Torres's dark hair and eyes appeared. B'Elanna stared. Father. It appeared that he'd been serious after all about wanting to stay in touch. She hadn't let herself believe it.

"Hello, B'Elanna," he said softly. "I got your letter. I'm glad you wrote me. It's so good to hear from you, know that you're well." He hesitated. "I have a lot of explaining to do. I hope you'll let me do it in person. I want so badly to see you again, to try to put things right . . . if they can be put right. If you don't want to see me, I'll understand. But I want to let you know that I love you, and that I'm sorry. Maybe you're old enough to understand that, and forgive me. I won't come to the banquet if you don't want me to. I'll wait to hear from you. If I don't . . . well, that's my answer, and I won't bother you again."

He blinked rapidly and his eyes looked very bright. "I love you, my little one. I hope to see you soon."

She felt Tom's arm around her, felt Admiral Paris's sympathetic gaze. She swallowed hard.

"Do you want to see him?" Tom asked, very softly.

"I—I don't know," she managed. She fumbled for the second message and handed it to Tom. "Let's see who this one's from."

Tom inserted the disk. A lovely but stern Klingon visage appeared, one Torres didn't recognize, and said, "I am Commander Logt. We must soon meet and speak of your mother. It is a matter of some urgency."

Torres recalled the words she and her mother had spoken in Grethor, the Klingon hell:

We will see each other again.

In Sto-Vo-Kor.

In Sto-Vo-Kor . . . *or maybe . . . when you get home.*

Perhaps this Logt knew what her mother had meant.

Janeway's heart lifted as Tuvok entered the room. Their eyes met, and he nodded. That was all she was going to get out of him, but it was enough. The *fal-tor-voh* had been successful. He would require regular, mild doses of medication to keep the disease from recurring, but the dreadful mental deterioration of which her future self had warned had been averted. How easily it had been accomplished; how devastating it would have been to watch this beloved friend fall to pieces slowly, irreversibly, in front of her eyes.

She permitted herself the briefest pang of envy. Both Paris and Tuvok had already gotten to see family members, and they had been in the Alpha Quadrant for only a few hours. Of course, each of their situations had been unique. Paris's father had been the head of this project and had been involved on a professional as well as a personal level. And getting Sek to his father had been a true medical emergency.

Even though the blue-green globe hovered tantalizingly in sight, they were traveling slowly on their way back to Earth, in order to get all the necessary red tape cut before their arrival. And, she thought, not to overwhelm her crew. Certainly, they wanted to get home and see their loved ones. But the whole thing had happened so suddenly, so unexpectedly, that it had been quite a shock. One of the first things Janeway requested, besides Sek's presence, was a counselor. Her request had been granted as well as she could wish. The *Enterprise* had sent its own counselor, one Deanna Troi, who had also apparently been at least peripherally involved with Project *Voyager.* Upon greeting the dark-haired, soft-spoken woman, Janeway had immediately felt confident in her abilities. Her crew was fortunate to have this capable woman to turn to.

Tuvok slipped quietly into a seat and everyone turned his or her attention to Admiral Paris.

The admiral didn't immediately launch into his speech. He took a moment to look at each of them in turn, smiling a little. Janeway was pleased to see his eyes linger affectionately on his new daughter-in-law. Torres had insisted on being present and the Doctor was keeping a close eye on her. Despite the slight risk, Janeway was glad she was here.

"There aren't words to articulate how happy I am to see you all here," Owen Paris began. "It's difficult to believe that in a short time you'll be home. We've been sending you information for some time, so you know about the Dominion War and its outcome. But there are some questions many of you, especially the former Maquis among you, must still be concerned about. I requested and was granted permission to be the one to give you the news.

"During the last days of the war there was a shortage of trained, capable officers. The situation was desperate. A general pardon was therefore offered to any of the Maquis who chose to return to Starfleet, absolving them of any wrongdoing, and after the massacre on Tevlik's moon, it was argued that there was no reason to doubt their commitment to the cause. To be honest, I opposed the amnesty. I did not think Maquis could be trusted. I have never been so happy to be proven wrong. The former Maquis served bravely and loyally. Therefore, I hereby extend the amnesty to all those who Captain Janeway informs me have served her so well."

Admiral Paris smiled, then spoke again. "Which means I'm spared the unpleasant duty of escorting my new daughter-in-law to prison."

There were smiles all around. Come to think of it, mused Janeway, there had been a lot of smiles on this ship over the last several hours. She met Chakotay's eyes. They hadn't spoken of it—there was no point; he knew that she would have to surrender him to the authorities if it came to that, although they both knew she'd fight tooth and nail to get his sentence commuted—but Janeway felt a fierce surge of joy to know that he, along with every other member of the crew, would be returning home a hero, not a prisoner.

"But it won't be a utopia to which you'll be returning, either," Admiral Paris continued. "War is never easy, but this one has truly been a hell to endure. It's taken a terrible toll on everyone. We lost millions of lives. We'll need all of you to pitch in and help us rebuild."

"You can count on us, Admiral," Janeway assured him.

"I'm sure I can," said the admiral. "After all, you

should be well rested—you've had a pretty long break."

There was a general chuckle, and Janeway knew the admiral meant nothing negative by the remark. Nonetheless, it stung. This hadn't been a seven-year picnic. They'd been in some terrible battles. She'd lost good people, and had suffered her own private pains at the things she'd been forced to do . . . and forced not to do.

At the same time, in a way they had been lucky. Who knew who would have survived and who wouldn't have, had they all been in the Alpha Quadrant during the Dominion War? Maybe she'd have lost even more crewmen. But maybe they could have made a difference, too. Shortened the war, somehow.

She shook off the thoughts, both the good and the bad. The situation was what it was. They were about to come home and, as the admiral had said, pitch in and help the Alpha Quadrant rebuild.

"And now," the admiral was saying, "there's someone else you need to meet."

The air beside him shimmered, and when the image solidified, Janeway saw the large-eyed, earnest Reginald Barclay. His face split into an enormous grin.

"Gosh," he said, "it's so good to finally get to see you all."

And regardless of what either Janeway or Admiral Paris had in mind, the room erupted into shouts and whoops as her well-trained, disciplined senior staff literally overturned chairs in order to embrace the man who had risked everything to bring them home.

Chapter

2

THE NEXT MORNING, WHEN JANEWAY MATERIALIZED in the transporter room of the *Enterprise,* she was pleased and flattered but not altogether surprised to see that none other than Captain Jean-Luc Picard was present to greet her.

"Permission to come aboard," she said lightly.

"Very happily granted," he replied, stepping forward with his hand outstretched. Janeway grasped it and swiftly covered it with her other hand.

"Kathryn," he said heartily, his hazel eyes warm with affection. "My God, it's good to see you. I could scarcely believe it when I saw *Voyager* soaring toward us out of that cloud of debris," he said. "We had been ready to fight the Borg, not welcome home a lost traveler."

"What can I say?" she quipped. "I like to make an entrance."

"Now that, you certainly did," said Picard. He extended an arm, indicating that she should precede him. "We had hoped you'd make it home one of these days. We just never imagined it would be quite so soon."

She smiled as they walked down the corridor to the turbolift. This whole meeting with Picard had a resonance that he could not possibly understand. Perhaps one day she'd tell him about the "fun" that Q had had with the two of them.

"I understand Reginald Barclay served with you before being assigned to Project *Voyager*," she said. "I must congratulate you. We'd still be quite a long way away if not for his diligence."

"Hard to believe that he used to be our problem child, isn't it?" Picard replied. "Yes, he's done us all proud. We've got a few moments before the, ah, 'Inquisition' begins. Would you care to join me in my ready room for a cup of coffee?"

She was pleased that he remembered her fondness for the beverage. She was about to accept when she thought about someone else who had a great deal to do with the fact that *Voyager* had made it safely home. That someone had given her life for all of them, and at the very least, she deserved a toast with her favorite beverage.

"Do you know," Janeway said, "I think I'd like to share a pot of Earl Grey with you instead. I have a hunch that I'm going to learn to like tea."

* * *

The debriefing began at 1300. Picard, Captains Rixx and DeSoto, and Admirals Paris, Brackett, Montgomery, and Amerman were present. Janeway was reminded of having to give her orals back at the Academy. Thanks to Barclay, *Voyager* had been able to transmit ship's logs covering several years, so Starfleet had already accessed much of what her crew had learned in the Delta Quadrant. If it had not been for that, Janeway imagined her debriefing alone would have taken days. As it was, there were only a few perfunctory questions, and when Janeway tried to elaborate, Montgomery, the admiral in charge, cut her off curtly each time.

Admiral Kenneth Montgomery had a long, lean face, tanned and weathered from what looked like years in the sun, and piercing gray eyes. With his thick, fair hair and muscular build, he could have been strikingly handsome, but there was an iciness about him that discouraged anything but the most professional, to-the-point interaction. She knew him by reputation only: He had been one of the key players in the war that had just recently ended. Janeway could easily see him in that role, and was grateful that Starfleet had had him.

But what did men like that do when there was peace?

More attention was given to *Voyager*'s interaction with the Borg. Even there, the questions were specific, and Janeway was none too gently urged to reply with equal specificity. Montgomery leaned forward when she began to speak of the most recent battle. From time to time, Janeway could see his jaw tensing.

"Now," Montgomery said when she had done, "aside

from your dealings with the Borg, where did you acquire this latest technology with which *Voyager* is equipped?"

She smiled a little. "Well, it's actually Starfleet technology. You just haven't figured it out yet."

Montgomery glared at her. "An official debriefing with three captains and four admirals is no place for jokes, Captain Janeway."

Her eyes narrowed. "I assure you, Admiral, I fully appreciate the seriousness of this matter. If I may be frank, I'm wondering if everyone here does. We seem to be racing through this debriefing when—"

"You say this is Starfleet technology, Captain," Montgomery interrupted. "Explain."

Choosing her words carefully to keep the explanation as brief as possible, Janeway explained about her future self returning to save *Voyager* and help them destroy the Borg transwarp hub. Montgomery's icy eyes flashed as she spoke and his jaw tightened, but he did not interrupt.

Janeway finished. There was a long, cold pause. Finally, Montgomery said in a flat voice, "Do you have any idea how many general orders you've violated, Captain?"

"Ken," said Paris gently, "first of all, she didn't do it. A twenty-six-year older version of her did. And besides, you've got to admit there are extenuating circumstances." The admiral's words were delivered in a calm and mild fashion, but his face was hard. Montgomery seemed about to retort, then nodded.

"We'll send over some of our best people and begin analyzing this ... this futuristic technology immediately. This hearing is over."

He picked up his padd and rose abruptly. Janeway, startled, met Picard's hazel eyes. He seemed as puzzled as she. Without any further interaction, Admiral Montgomery strode out and was followed by several others. Picard and Paris remained as Janeway gathered her notes.

"Admiral Paris," she said, "permission to speak freely."

He looked troubled, but replied, "Granted."

Janeway put her hands on her hips and stuck her chin out. "That entire briefing lasted less than an hour," she said to them. "We've been gone for seven years. We've accumulated data on over four hundred completely new species. We've had more interaction with the Borg than anyone in this quadrant, and we've managed to beat them nearly every time. We've successfully liberated a humanoid boy and a human woman who was assimilated when she was six years old. We've got an EMH who's exceeded his programming far beyond expected parameters, and we've got an entire crew that has performed not just well, but *exceptionally*. And Starfleet gets all it wants to know in under an hour?"

She was aware that her words were irate, almost belligerent, but she'd been given permission to speak her mind. It was Picard who answered first.

"It's going to be difficult for you to understand this, Kathryn, but ... while everyone in Starfleet knows about your adventure, and is delighted that you made it safely home despite the incredible odds, you aren't going to be as feted as you might have been had the war not happened."

"It's not that people don't care," put in Paris. "It's

that there are so many things we need to be doing to recover. Our resources have been depleted throughout the quadrant. We're helping the Cardassians rebuild, mourning our dead, trying to move on."

"I do understand, Admiral. But the things we've learned can help you do that."

"And they will," said Picard. "Everything we'll need to learn is in your computer databanks. The information will be passed on directly to the experts in their field. The board simply didn't need to keep you here for hours when everyone, including you, has other things to do."

They were trying to soften the blow, of course, and she was going to let them think they had succeeded. "Speaking of which," she said, forcing a smile, "I'd better get back to my ship. Thank you, gentlemen, and good day."

In about a half hour, *Voyager* was going to be crawling with Starfleet personnel whose job it was to learn everything about all the modifications that had been made on the ship in the last seven years, particularly the new technology that Admiral Janeway had given them. As she stood in the turbolift en route to Holodeck One, Janeway wondered why the modifications seemed to take priority over all the other things *Voyager* had brought back with it. The tactical information on the Borg should have been the most vital information, not the shielding technology and other improvements.

The turbolift halted, and she sighed. She was not looking forward to this, but it had to be done. One of the things the Starfleet engineers would analyze would be all the holodeck simulations. Janeway had told her crew that anything they regarded as "personal" could and should be deleted.

The doors to the holodeck hissed open and she entered. Laughter and music reached her ears, and she smiled despite herself.

"Katie, darling!" cried Michael Sullivan, drying his hands with a dish towel. His handsome face was alight with affection. Before she knew it, he'd caught her around the waist, whirled her around twice, and planted a kiss on her mouth. "I've missed you."

"I've missed you too, Michael." Gently, she disengaged herself from his strong arms. "I have some sad news. I won't be able to come to Fair Haven again."

It hurt her, to watch the light fade from his eyes. "Your journey . . . you've made it home then, have you?" At her nod, he said, "Why, Katie, that's wonderful. Just grand. You've been trying for so long. I'm happy for you."

And he was, she had no doubt. But she was sorry for herself. Tenderly, she reached out and touched his cheek, feeling the warmth of his holographic skin, the scratch of his holographic beard stubble. He wasn't real, but in a way, he had become very real to her. She had learned to care for him, but where she was going, there was once again a chance for her to learn to care for a living, breathing person.

She stood on tiptoe to kiss him, sweetly, gently, whispered, "Good-bye," then turned and left. She had instructed the computer not to accept any more adjustments to Michael Sullivan from her. It would be up to

Tom Paris, the designer of the program, to save or delete the program as he chose.

But as far as she was concerned, when the doors closed behind her, she had left Fair Haven and all it meant—laughter, freedom from responsibility, a simpler way of living—behind.

And she was surprised at just how painful it was.

The Doctor looked up in surprise as Seven of Nine entered sickbay. She did not appear to be in a good mood. However, with Seven, that was usually a given.

"Implants acting up?" he asked.

"Negative," she replied, then looked a bit discomfited. "I . . . wished to inquire if you needed any assistance."

"My sickbay rush has come and gone," he replied. "Actually, the only thing I'm doing now is writing up my report for Starfleet."

She inclined her blond head. "In that case, I shall leave." Seven turned and strode toward the door.

"Seven, wait a minute," he called after her. She halted. "What about you? I'm certain you will have an extensive report as well, considering your unique position among the crew."

Apparently that was the wrong thing to say. Seven all but glowered. "I completed my report. And I have also been debriefed."

"How was that?" Poor child, he thought. They had probably raked her over the coals, grilled her on everything conceivable.

"It was brief," she replied.

The Doctor considered letting her know that she'd

come close to making a pun, then let it pass. "I'm surprised," he said.

"Yes," she said archly. "As am I. Apparently, my 'unique position' warrants no more than forty-five minutes of Starfleet's time." She paused. "Icheb has received notification that he has been accepted into Starfleet Academy."

"Seven, that's wonderful! You must be very proud of him."

"I am."

"But you're going to miss him, aren't you?"

She nodded. "I had not fully taken into account what returning to Earth really means. We will all be . . . scattered. I had not anticipated that Icheb and I would be separated quite so soon."

He wondered where Chakotay fit into all this, but said nothing. "And of course Naomi . . ."

"Naomi Wildman will be returning to her home, to live with both father and mother. It is an appropriate end result."

"But you've been very close to both these children. You're experiencing what some people call 'empty-nest syndrome.' You've got nothing to do in astrometrics, and I know what fulfillment you get out of your work. And on top of it all, you have also never been certain of where you were going to fit in once you return home." He grimaced a little. "Neither am I."

She regarded him thoughtfully. If he had had a heart, it would have raced. Even though he knew that her affections were given elsewhere, the Doctor realized that his infatuation with Seven was not going to go away.

"Would you care for an ice-cream sundae?" she asked. He smiled. "I'd love one."

"I don't want to go home," Naomi Wildman stated flatly. Counselor Deanna Troi was surprised at the vehemence she was sensing from the child.

"I don't blame you," Troi responded, clearly surprising Naomi. "You were born here. *Voyager* is your home."

"You understand," said Naomi, brightening. "I have Mama, Seven, Icheb . . . I don't need a father."

"But you might like to have one," Troi offered.

"Everyone expects me to be so happy about meeting my father, but I'm not. I'm . . . I'm scared. Ktarians are scary-looking."

"Your mother wasn't scared of him. She thought him a wonderful person. Good enough to marry and be the father of her child."

Naomi made a face and looked down at her feet, dangling a few inches off the floor. Deanna waited patiently, but Naomi remained silent.

"You know," Deanna finally said, "we have a lot in common, only backward." Curious, Naomi looked up. "My father was with me until I was seven years old. You aren't going to get to meet your father until you're already seven, but you're luckier than I am. You see, my father died when I was your age. He never got to see me grow up, graduate from the Academy, learn to be a counselor. There was so much in my life that I wished he had been there for, but he wasn't."

Naomi had stopped fidgeting. Her eyes were fixed on Troi's.

"You've got all that time ahead with your daddy. Hasn't he sent you letters about how anxious he is to meet you?"

Naomi nodded.

"He probably thinks he's the luckiest man in the universe. Not only is he getting his wife back, whom he loves very much, but he's getting a beautiful, smart daughter, too."

A shy, soft smile curved Naomi's lips.

"You don't have to love him right away. Love takes time. But don't you think you could try to like him?"

Naomi thought. "I suppose," she said. "I just wish he could have met Uncle Neelix."

"Neelix helped shape the girl you've grown into, Naomi. So in a way, your father *will* get to meet Neelix. And you will never lose your uncle. He will always be part of you."

And at that, the girl rewarded Troi with the biggest smile she'd seen yet from her.

Chapter 3

TROI SMILED TIREDLY as Captain Picard handed her a dish of ice cream. "I need this after today," she said, spooning up a bite.

"How many people did you speak to?" he asked, then turned to the replicator. "Tea. Earl Grey. Hot."

"About thirty," she said.

He raised an eyebrow. "That's more than you're supposed to see outside of catastrophic situations," he reprimanded, taking his tea and sitting beside her.

"In a way, it is a catastrophic situation," Troi replied. "These people have been without a professional counselor for seven full years, Captain. And they've been through some incredible adventures—some wondrous, some brutally tragic. They've been tremendously isolated, and they've adapted by creating their own little world aboard that ship."

"Good or bad?"

She smiled. "Very good. Captain Janeway has almost assumed the rank of a god in some eyes. And after some of the stories I've heard today, that designation seems quite believable."

"Hmm," Picard said.

"And now, with no warning, no time to prepare, to mentally ready themselves for it, they've achieved their goal. They made it back to the Alpha Quadrant. They're going to be with their families in a week." She paused. "Thank you, by the way, for recommending to the admirals that we not travel home at top speed. *Voyager*'s crew desperately needs the extra time to readjust."

He nodded. "As I suspected. Do you think there will be trouble? Any former Maquis returning with fire in the belly? There was probably a lot of desire for revenge when they heard about the decimation of Tevlik's moonbase."

She shook her dark head and took another bite of ice cream. "No. The division of Federation and Maquis has long since faded. But I do think it likely that they might think of themselves as *Voyager* crewmen first, and Starfleet officers and enlisted second."

"That could be a problem." He leaned back, thinking. "Even Janeway, who's a sterling example of what a captain should be, didn't seem to fully grasp how much things had changed—though, frankly, Admiral Montgomery was unnecessarily harsh with her. It's a shame, really. At any other time in recent history *Voyager*'s homecoming would be the most important thing to happen to Starfleet in any given year. Now their safe return is barely a footnote."

Troi's large, dark eyes were somber as she regarded her captain. "Some of them are beginning to understand that. And it's not helping their readjustment any."

"I can imagine." He made his decision. "Tomorrow, I want you back on *Voyager* for the duration of its trip back to Earth. Those people are going to need you. You have my permission to regard this as a catastrophic-level duty assignment."

"Aye, sir." She answered quickly enough, and he was certain that she was more than willing to help, but he also knew these next few days were going to be difficult for her.

"And Deanna," he said, teasing gently, "it's not going to be easy. Better fortify yourself with more chocolate."

Janeway sat in her ready room, pondering. The days had passed more quickly than she had imagined. In sixteen hours, they would be in orbit around Earth. She and her senior staff had all been debriefed. Torres's had taken the longest—four hours. Janeway had the dubious honor of coming in second. Everyone else had been dismissed after a half hour or forty-five minutes. Hardly enough for an extended away mission, let alone one that had lasted seven years. . . .

Stop it, she told herself. *What did you expect? Medals? A parade down the streets of San Francisco? Fireworks? These people are coming off a brutal war. Be grateful that you got so many home safely. You didn't do this to win praise, you did this to keep a promise—to return your crew to their families.*

Her door chimed. "Come," she called.

Chakotay entered. He was clad in his dress uniform, as was she. "It's time," he said.

Janeway had thought about doing this via intercom, but decided that she wanted to do it in person. So her entire crew was assembled in Cargo Bay Two. They were all clad in dress uniform. Some of them wore medals. She let Chakotay precede her, heard the tinny whistle announcing her entrance.

"Captain on deck!"

The crew snapped to attention. Janeway savored the picture, her eyes roaming from one individual to the next. This was going to be bittersweet. She strode to the front of the room and stood behind the podium.

"At ease," she said. They relaxed. She looked at the padd she held in her hand, then carefully placed it down. Even though she had spent hours crafting the speech, she now realized she didn't want to use it. She would speak from the heart. Her crew deserved it.

"Seven years ago, I made a decision that left this crew and this fine ship stranded thousands of light-years from everything we knew. Even then, I held a firm conviction that this day, today, would come. The day when we are but a few hours away from Earth, and from finally seeing our loved ones. We have faced many challenges, learned many things. We've lost some fine people. Too many."

She paused, giving herself and her crew a moment to reflect on the sacrifices some of their number had made. The losses still ached. If she were honest with herself, she'd have to admit, it would have been impossible to get every single crewman home while battling such odds. But oh, how she had wanted to. Her eyes found Icheb and little Naomi, Gilmore and Lessing from the *Equinox*. She smiled, heartened by the sight of their faces.

"And added some new crew members along the way. Each of you has contributed in so many ways to making this incredible journey the astounding feat it was. It has been a true honor to be your captain. I have asked and asked, and asked yet more from you, and you always continued to astonish and amaze me with your resourcefulness, your courage, and your compassion. But now, the journey is done. This unique voyage has, finally, ended. We have come home."

Her throat closed up and she blinked hard. She reached for the padd, found the spot she wanted. "I'd like to close with a quote from the Earth author, T. S. Eliot. 'Not fare well, but fare forward, voyagers.' " She looked out into the sea of faces, all known, all loved, and knew that she would miss them and this ship desperately. "May we, voyagers all, fare forward. Godspeed."

The room erupted in applause. She saw that her mixture of pain and joy was reflected on almost all the faces of her crew. Many were weeping openly. Chakotay stepped forward and motioned for quiet.

"Captain," he said, "if you can spare the time, the crew has a request. They would all like the opportunity to make their personal farewells to you now, while they are all still formally crew members of *Voyager*."

Janeway had thought her heart full, but now it overflowed. For the rest of her life, she knew, she would remember this: walking down the seemingly endless line, sharing laughter, hugs, handshakes, slaps on the back. She tried to brand every face into her brain, every word, every expression. Whatever her own new voyage held for her, it would be hard-pressed to measure up to the exquisite, painful joy of this single precious moment.

There was to be a "welcome home" dinner for all crew members and their guests held at Starfleet headquarters in San Francisco. Because this was a hugely complicated gathering to arrange at such short notice, all crew were requested not to leave the ship in order to greet family and friends until the dinner.

"This is driving me nuts," Harry Kim confided to Paris, stalking up and down the small room like a caged animal. "Why can't I see them?"

"Starfleet red tape. That's one thing I haven't missed in the last seven years," said Paris, cooing at little Miral. She wasn't buying it. She glared at him, then opened her mouth and wailed lustily. He rose and thrust Miral into Harry's arms. "Here. I don't want to let all that rhythmic, soothing pacing go to waste."

"You're lucky," said Kim, cradling the baby awkwardly and almost shouting to be heard over her crying. "You got to see your dad before anyone else on this ship."

"Yeah, but it could have gone worse," said Paris. He grinned a little as Miral's angry cries faded into satisfied murmuring. "And don't forget, I'm getting to meet a Klingon father-in-law tonight."

"And how is that worse than any other kind of father-in-law?" challenged B'Elanna, coming out of the bathroom adjusting her dress uniform. "Hey, Starfleet, you're pretty good with her. Too bad you won't be around to baby-sit anymore."

Kim smiled, feeling a rush of affection for both of these people. The terms he and B'Elanna had used, which had once marked their differences, had become pet names between two dear friends.

"Don't worry, Maquis," he said. "I hope to visit you guys often."

"Door's always open, Harry." He rose and took his daughter from Harry's arms, then turned to B'Elanna. "Showtime," he said.

"Seven, what are you doing here?" said the Doctor, adjusting his dress uniform. "I thought that you and Chakotay would already be at the party."

"Commander Chakotay will be anxious for some time alone with his Maquis friends. I will not be attending," she said stiffly. "I have come to complete the cataloguing I began earlier." As if she were the head of sickbay and not he, Seven slipped easily into the Doctor's chair.

"What about your aunt? Surely she'll be there tonight."

"I received a transmission from her. She is unwell and also will be unable to attend." Seven's fingers were flying over the controls, but now they paused in their frantic motions. "She has extended an invitation for me to stay with her once I am . . . settled in."

"Seven," the Doctor said gently, "please tell me you

are going to accept." Seven did not answer. "She's the only family you have!"

"*Voyager* was my family," she blurted before she could retract the statement. A blush colored her cheeks. "And now my family is dispersed. There is no purpose to my attending tonight, and these catalogues—"

"Are what we call busywork and are almost completely superfluous," the Doctor said firmly. "And there is actually quite a vital purpose to your attending tonight."

Surprised, she looked up at him. "What?"

"Have you never thought that I don't have any family, either?" he said. "Oh, I'm certain I'll soon be hugely sought-after in the medical community, with my vast store of knowledge and experience. But tonight, it's all about friends and family. I won't have anyone to talk to at the banquet."

He extended an arm. "I would be honored if you would grant me the favor of your company this evening, Miss Seven of Nine."

For a long, long moment, he thought she would refuse. He expected her to refuse, actually. But finally, an uncertain smile curved her full lips, and that smile reached her eyes.

"I will require a change of uniform," she said.

Kim materialized in an enormous hall. Flags representing every Federation member planet hung from the high, arched ceiling. Windows that ran almost the entire length of the walls opened to the San Francisco sky, and the muted hues of twilight vied with artificial lighting for the right to illuminate this vast chamber. Soft music played in the background, and more tables than Kim had ever seen in one place stretched the length of this great hall.

Kim gaped openly for a moment. He had never seen this room before; it was reserved for high ceremony. He supposed that Starfleet had, after the cursory briefings, come to the realization that *Voyager* rated such kudos. Quickly, though, he forgot about the opulence of the room and began scanning the crowd, looking for those whose faces he had kept in his mind for seven years.

So many people! Out of the corner of his eye, he saw big, jolly Chell squeal happily as he rushed to embrace two blue Bolians. Little Naomi, standing close beside a beaming Samantha Wildman, formally stuck her hand out to a towering Ktarian male, who gently accepted it. Vorik stood politely conversing with three Vulcans. They appeared to be strangers, but, knowing Vulcans, Kim was willing to bet they were his family.

Captain Janeway was hugging two women at the same time. One was an older woman who looked a lot like her, and the other was a little younger than she. They had to be her mother and sister.

Over there was Chakotay, his expression a mixture of joy and sorrow, as he embraced men and women who Kim assumed were fellow Maquis members. And there was the Paris family. Kim didn't recognize the older, attractive woman, but guessed she was Tom's mother. Standing next to them was a tall, handsome man with black hair and a dark complexion.

Harry stared. Was this B'Elanna's father, after all these years? B'Elanna looked as if she were trying to decide whether to punch the man or throw herself in his arms.

He never saw which she did, because at that moment, a beloved voice cried, "Harry! Oh, Harry!"

Harry whirled and saw an elderly Asian couple threading their way through the crowd. When their eyes met, the woman lifted a long, rectangular box over her head. He knew what it was, and tears sprang to his eyes. She had brought his clarinet.

"Mom! Dad!" he cried, and rushed to embrace them fiercely. And even as he hugged them, he saw another person he had never forgotten, despite the intervening years, the resignation at never seeing her again, and the things he had shared with other women who had entered his life. He saw a lovely face framed by curly dark hair, and large eyes filled with tears even as her mouth curved wide in a smile of joy.

Libby.

Voyager's crew had all finally come home.

Chapter

4

WHEN SEVEN OF NINE AND THE DOCTOR MATERIALIZED in the hall, Chakotay did a double take. What was she doing here? She had said she hadn't wanted to come. And now here she was, her long golden hair down about her shoulders, wearing the soft, flowing red dress he so admired on her. Their eyes met for an instant; then she looked away.

More than Chakotay noted her presence. Almost at once, a murmuring arose from the crowd, and conversation slowed for an instant. Seven kept her head high, her visage almost haughty, but her cheeks reddened. Chakotay knew at once what she was thinking. She was trying to be brave, to not appear intimidated, and inwardly fighting a desire to flee. No doubt, at this moment she was probably wishing she *had* stayed on board after all.

"Is that Seven of Nine?" Sveta said. "Wow. You always did have good taste in women, Chakotay. Except for that time when you dated a Cardassian spy."

Her warm, rich voice was full of good humor; it was gentle teasing, nothing more, but it bothered Chakotay. He forced a smile.

"Excuse me," he said, and headed for Seven before the rest could descend on her.

He was too late. Already she had drawn a crowd. They closed in on her like a pack of hungry wolves, and Chakotay could see her blue eyes widen, her breath quicken, as she tried in vain to step backward. She drew closer to the Doctor, who was behaving like a father with a daughter.

"Yes, yes, I know you're all fascinated by Seven," he was saying, "but she's already had her debriefing. If you want to talk to someone, talk to me."

But they didn't want the Doctor, they wanted Seven. Chakotay couldn't believe it. These were all families of other crewmen. Good people, he was sure. Why then were they behaving like the paparazzi of old Earth, actually reaching out to touch Seven as though she were some kind of—

"Ladies and gentlemen," came a cool, female voice he knew very well. "Seven isn't used to all this attention. You know her story. I ask you to please give her a little time to adjust."

Small though she was, Janeway smoothly threaded her way with ease through the press of people to stand beside Seven. She slipped an arm about the younger woman's waist and smiled at the crowd. It was a pleasant expression, but there was steel in that smile. Mama Janeway wasn't about to let anyone hurt her cub.

The crowd drew back. Janeway's appeal to their better natures had worked, at least for the moment. Chakotay was certain, though, that people would find some excuse or other to "drop by" Seven's place at the table during the course of the dinner.

Politely but inexorably, Janeway steered Seven to a corner. The Doctor accompanied them, trotting beside them like an attentive dog, concern radiating from him. Janeway reached for a glass of champagne, thought better of it, and selected a glass of juice instead. She handed it to Seven. Chakotay smothered a smile. Seven would be better off if she didn't touch a drop of alcohol tonight.

He finally managed to reach them. "Seven, I'm so sorry," he said. "If you'd let me know that you had changed your mind about coming—"

"It's quite all right, Commander," she said, chilling him with the formal title. "I changed my mind at the last minute. I had no wish to intrude upon your reunion with old friends." Her eyes lingered on the slim, beautiful form of Sveta as she spoke.

He stared at her, his heart sinking. How could she possibly think that her presence would be an intrusion? Would he ever understand this complex woman?

Chakotay decided it was time to cut to the chase on this. Firmly but gently, in a manner that brooked no argument, he clasped Seven's elbow.

"Excuse us for a moment," he said to Janeway and the Doctor. Before she could protest, he had steered her away. "That had to be awful," he said before she could speak. "As I said, if you'd let me know you'd changed your mind, I could have helped prevent it somewhat."

Her eyes were like chips of blue ice. "That is not necessary, Commander. It would appear that on Earth, I will need to learn to fight my own battles. I will not cower behind my—"

She closed her mouth, not finishing the sentence. What had she been going to say? "My lover"? "My friend"? "My commanding officer"?

He released his hold on her elbow. "Seven, this is me," he said, softly. "Please don't shut me out. I want to be there for you."

She glanced away. "I know."

"But you don't want me there." His voice was sad, but not surprised.

She looked back up at him. "Admiral Janeway said that you and I would get married in the future."

He smiled. "You know, somehow that stuck in my mind."

"But that was a future on *Voyager*. Not here."

His smile faded. The ache in his heart pained him, but it also had a sense of inevitability about it. He didn't want to hear any more, but she grimly pressed on, as if now that she had started, she had to say it all.

"*Voyager* was my collective. I knew I was safe there. I trusted all of you; I knew all of you. I could . . . I could try to learn to love. But all that's changed. We've returned to Earth. I'm a—an oddity."

"Seven, that's not true, you're—"

"And I have to learn to find my place again. I knew who I was on *Voyager*. Here, I have no idea."

He took a deep breath. The irony didn't escape him. He had cared for three women on *Voyager*—Seska, Janeway, and Seven of Nine. One was a madwoman, a traitor, whose "yes" had never been real. The second had told him "no" gently and sweetly, because they were together on *Voyager*. And the third was telling him "no" because they *weren't* together on *Voyager*. It was kind of funny, in a painful way.

"Can't win for losing," he said ruefully, chuckling despite his hurt.

She frowned slightly. "I do not understand," she said.

"No, I suppose you wouldn't. It's okay, Seven. You're right. You need to learn who you are, and you need to do that without me coming along for the ride."

He wanted to kiss her one last time, but he felt the myriad eyes upon them. So he contented himself with gently stroking her cheek, smiled at her, and let her go.

B'Elanna was surprised at how small her father appeared to her. To her as a child, he had been such a large, comforting presence; and when he had gone, his absence had been even more enormous. Now he seemed to be just human-sized. Not a god, not a demon; just a man. She recalled a man with shiny black hair; now that hair, though still thick, was more gray than black. There were wrinkles around his face that did not jibe with her memories, and a stiffness to his movements that pained her to see.

Her father was growing old.

John Torres was still fit and healthy for his age, but she had not watched him grow older gradually. This was a startling change to B'Elanna, one that she had glimpsed but not fully integrated when she had talked to him briefly on *Voyager*.

The way he was staring at her told her that she, too, had changed. Probably more than he. But children grew up, and parents grew old, and that was the way of the universe, wasn't it? What did the universe care that one little half-Klingon woman grieved the death of her mother, and the aging of her father, and mourned even more deeply the opportunities for joy that the ill-fated triangle had missed?

Cradled in her mother's arms, Miral made a soft, squawking noise. It broke the uncomfortable pause that had ensued after the first stiff round of greetings had been exchanged. At once, B'Elanna's attention was diverted from father to child.

"May I hold her?" John Torres asked.

Not trusting her voice, B'Elanna nodded. As she placed Miral in her grandfather's arms, B'Elanna's body briefly touched her father's. It was the first touch they had exchanged in years, and it felt like a shock passed through them.

Daddy.

And then the instant of physical warmth was gone, and John Torres was smiling down at his granddaughter. "She's beautiful," he said softly. "I am so sorry her namesake couldn't be here."

Out of the corner of her eye, she saw Tom open his mouth to speak. Before he could say anything, and before she could lose her courage, B'Elanna blurted, "How did my mother die?"

"So much for small talk," Tom muttered.

Torres's eyes flickered from the baby to his daughter. He looked dreadfully uncomfortable. For a moment, the thought flared in B'Elanna's mind: *Good. He should be uncomfortable.*

"I don't know."

She stared at him. All the warmth that she had been feeling for him turned to ice.

"How the hell can you not—"

"B'Elanna," John said softly but firmly, "they never found the body. Your mother went on some sort of, I don't know, some Klingon ritual. She never came back and was declared dead a year ago per Klingon law. I only learned about it myself quite recently. We—we weren't in close contact."

Shame washed over B'Elanna and she felt her cheeks grow hot. She was acutely aware of the Parises standing awkwardly by, trying to be present and yet not intervene. Tom had been right. Small talk would have been better.

There was not even a word in the Klingon language for "small talk."

"I'm sorry," she said. "It's just that—"

"B'Elanna, dear," said Mrs. Paris, "it's all right. Everyone understands. You've had quite an adjustment to make and there's so much that's changed. Of course you're going to be off-balance for a little while."

The human woman reached as if to take her daughter-in-law's hand, then seemed to think better of it. Before Julia could withdraw, B'Elanna reached out and clasped the other woman's extended hand. A smile spread across Julia's still-lovely face.

"B'Elanna received a message from someone named

Commander Logt," Tom said. "It was pretty cryptic. She said she needed to talk to B'Elanna about her mother, and that it was kind of urgent."

John Torres frowned. "That name rings a bell," he said. "Though I can't imagine why she'd want to talk about Miral as if it was urgent."

B'Elanna dropped Julia's hand. "I have to talk to her," said B'Elanna. She surged forward to leave, but Tom's hand closed about her upper arm.

"Sweetheart," he said, "the banquet is only going to be a couple of hours. I promise, we'll send a message to this Logt the minute it's over."

She turned angrily, a sharp retort on her lips, but it died when she saw the pleading in his blue eyes. *It's my mother we're talking about!* she wanted to scream.

But it was also her father they were talking about, and he was right here, warm and alive. And it was Tom's mother, and Tom's father. The strange experience—she couldn't call it a dream—about encountering her mother on the Barge of the Dead was always in her mind. But she was not the child John Torres remembered, willful and headstrong and rash. B'Elanna Torres still had her Klingon passion and pride embedded in her genes, but she had learned patience.

Well, she amended with a rueful smile, she was at least *learning* patience.

She nodded at Tom. She would stay for the banquet. Stay, and learn about who this father was now.

Libby Webber was even more beautiful than Harry Kim remembered. He was of course delighted to be reunited with his mom and dad; Harry was an only child, born late to these elderly parents and therefore all the more precious to them. He loved them fiercely, but he was a man now, not a little boy, and although he tried to be the dutiful son and pay those who bore him the attention and deference they deserved, damned if his head didn't keep swinging around as if pulled to the woman standing across from him.

Had her eyes sparkled so brightly seven years ago? Was her hair that curly and thick, her smile that wide? He desperately wished he could talk with her alone, ask her how she had been, *really* been. Was there anyone else? There was no ring on her finger, but that didn't rule out a serious boyfriend. Or girlfriend, for that matter—Harry wasn't narrow-minded in his distressing scenarios of imagining Libby attached. They laughed and talked, but it was all shallow, all surface. If only they could speak deeply, as they used to, speak to and from the heart.

His feelings for her surprised him. There had certainly been other women in the intervening seven years. And they hadn't been flings, either. Unlike some men he'd known, Harry knew that where his body went, his heart followed. Recollecting some of the things he had done, had felt, even now Harry felt a pang of loss. Once, he had believed in the very romantic concept that there was only one Someone for everyone, one true soul mate. He knew better now. Love—real love, not infatuation or passion—could be shared with more than one person in a lifetime.

She was watching him keenly, and as the shadows settled on his heart, she cocked her head in a gesture that was deeply familiar to him. Libby smiled, slowly, that wide, all-encompassing smile that had always made him feel like he was dancing on air.

"You've changed a lot, Harry," she said softly. "I can see it in your eyes. You've really grown up."

"Don't I know it," his mother sighed, seemingly unaware of the electric connection between her son and his former fiancée. "Just yesterday he was little Harry, singing in the sunshine with me. My baby boy." She reached up and tousled his hair. Harry knew from experience that it was now standing straight up and he blushed, embarrassed.

"Ma," he said, drawing the word out in exasperation as he tried to smooth his ruffled hair.

Libby laughed. "It *is* good to see you again," she said.

Throwing caution to the wind, knowing he'd hear about it all through dinner and probably beyond, Harry turned to address his parents. "Excuse us for a moment," he said, grabbed Libby's hand, and pulled the startled woman toward a corner of the hall where they could talk.

"Harry," she protested. "Your parents are going to be furious!"

"Let them be. They've got me for the rest of tonight and probably for a long time after that. I don't—I don't know how much time we're going to have."

He realized that he was still clutching her hand and released her. Libby clasped both hands behind her back. Not a good sign, Harry thought.

"Well, what do you want to talk about?"

He stared into her eyes. What *did* he want to talk

about? What could they, separated for seven years, even have to talk about?

He knew what he wanted to say and do. He wanted to reach out to her, grasp her hands, and say, *Libby, there have been other women. I'm sure that you've been with other men. We didn't know if we'd ever see each other again. I'm not ashamed of what I've done, but now I've come home. And I see you again, and it's as if I've never been away, and as if I've been gone for a thousand years. Is there someone else now? Could you learn to care for me . . . love me again? Is there anything left of love for me in you?*

He said, "How've you been?" and hated himself.

She fixed him with a skeptical gaze. "I can't believe you dragged me over here and annoyed your parents just to ask me how I've been," she said, challenging him.

He said, "No, really, how've you been?" and hated himself even more.

Libby regarded him appraisingly for a moment longer, and then said, "Good. I've been good, Harry. My career's really taken off and I perform at concerts all over the quadrant now. I've become a vegetarian and I've never felt healthier. I've dated several men, slept with a few, and fallen in love with one. It didn't last. I live in a cabin by the sea where I have to balance my love for the ocean with the mess the humidity makes of my Ktarian *lal-shak*. I have two cats and a rabbit named Binky. That answer your question?"

Harry's face felt as hot as if he were standing next to a bonfire. "I'm sorry," he stammered. "I guess you shouldn't have come."

"Silly me," she said, heat entering her voice, "I thought you might want to see me, for old times' sake. Guess you're all grown up now and don't have time for women you once said you loved. So, Harry, how've *you* been?"

"Now you're angry," he said. "I'm so stupid. I thought—hell, I don't know what I thought." As furious with himself now as she was, he made to move past her. She blocked him, placing her hand on his chest. It was warm and strong and stopped him as surely as if he had run into a forcefield.

"I cried my eyes out when they said your ship was lost," she said softly. They didn't look at one another. Her gaze was on the floor, his straight ahead. Her hand was still on his chest, fingers spread wide, and he wondered if she could feel how fast his heart was racing. He was certain she could.

"I waited for news. Any news. Good or bad. Anything that would let me move on, one way or another. And when it finally came, I cried again. Then I dried my eyes and got on with my life. I put all my pain and passion into my music, and it took my talent to a place it had never been before. Every time I played, you were in my thoughts, Harry Kim. I hoped that you had died quickly, without pain. I started seeing people, opening my heart up again. And then I heard from your parents that they were getting messages from you. *Messages,* Harry. *Voyager* was making it home as best it could, and you were alive, and you were sending your parents messages, but there weren't any for me."

His heart breaking, Harry risked a look down at her. Tears glittered like diamonds in her long, thick lashes.

She still stared at the floor. He wanted to speak, but didn't dare.

"So I figured you'd forgotten. Didn't want to see me. Your parents insisted I come here, and you know what, you were right. I shouldn't have."

"Libby," he said in a hoarse whisper. "Oh, God. I was afraid to contact you. I was afraid to find out that you were married, or hated me, or, I don't know. I was just scared. There have been other people for me too. I'll be honest, there have been some women I've really loved. But there was never anyone who . . . who fit with me the way you did. There's no one now."

In a small voice, she said, "There's no one now for me either."

Swallowing hard, aware that they were in a crowd of people, Harry stepped in front of her and turned her face up to his. Her eyes were brimming with tears. How many times had he gazed into those eyes before bending to kiss those full, soft lips?

"I don't know about you, but I think there's still something here between us," he said, risking all.

She nodded. "There is," she admitted.

"What do you want to do about it?"

She smiled, and to Harry it was as if the sun had broken out from behind a cloud bank. "I want to watch your parents revel in having their only son home safe and sound. I want to eat every bite of what is no doubt going to be a scrumptious feast. I want to split dessert with you like we always did. I want to take a walk in the moonlight and hold your hand and see how that feels."

He felt his own lips stretch in a grin and knew he looked like an idiot. A very happy idiot.

"Sounds like a plan."

A clinking sound interrupted his thoughts. Someone was tapping on a glass with a fork. The crowd quieted and turned their attention toward their host, Admiral Paris. Although he presented quite a formal appearance, clad as he was in his dress uniform, the admiral's face was alight with pleasure.

"Ladies and gentlemen," he said, "this banquet is going to serve a double purpose. Not only are we able to finally welcome back our husbands and wives, sons and daughters, brothers and sisters once thought lost, we have an opportunity to recognize some of those for special achievement during that incredible seven-year journey. Will the following people step forward: Ensign Lyssa Campbell. Ensign Vorik. Ensign Harry Kim."

Surprised, Harry glanced down at Libby. She pushed him forward. "Well, go on!" she said, grinning impishly.

He moved forward to step beside Lyssa and Vorik. Lyssa was almost bouncing up and down, her blue eyes bright. Vorik, of course, was as composed as a good son of Vulcan ought to be.

"You know what this is about?" Lyssa whispered.

"Nope," Harry shot back.

Paris was continuing to recite names. Harry saw Tom and B'Elanna step forward, along with their captain. They formed a line and stood at attention before Admiral Paris. An aide appeared beside him, carrying a small box.

"At ease," Paris said. "This is a bit impromptu, but it's the best we could do on such short notice, and we certainly didn't want to wait. Captain Janeway, please step forward."

She did so. The aide opened the small wooden box. Nestled against the lush purple of velvet were several pips. Harry took a quick, sharp breath as he realized what was coming.

"For your determination in getting your crew home despite almost impossible odds—and for beating the Borg at their own game—you are hereby promoted to admiral."

Something flickered in Janeway's eyes and then was gone. Harry thought he knew what it was. Admiral. No more ship. Just a desk job. It might have been an advancement in rank, but for Janeway, Kim knew it was a demotion to the soul.

He also thought she might be thinking of the Admiral Janeway who had crossed the barrier of time itself to help them return home at the cost of her life. That had to be a bittersweet association. Nonetheless, the new admiral smiled as if it pleased her no end.

Paris went down the row. Both Lieutenants Paris and Torres became lieutenant commanders. And Kim, Vorik, and Campbell turned to face the applause of the crowd as lieutenants. He couldn't help but glance in Libby's direction. She was clapping wildly.

"And now," said Paris, "it's my understanding that the chefs have been waiting seven years to prepare this particular welcome-home banquet. Let's not keep them waiting any longer."

To Libby, the banquet seemed to drag on forever. When, finally, it wound down and the Kims asked

Libby to join them for tea at their home, she declined as politely as possible. She made certain that there was not a chance for her to be truly alone with the young lieutenant. She wasn't ready for that yet. So she hugged his parents good-bye, smiled with what she hoped was shy sincerity at Harry, and agreed to meet him for lunch tomorrow.

When she materialized in her own small seaside cabin, she breathed an enormous sigh of relief. Her cats, Indigo and Rowena, meowed with annoyance. It was well past their dinnertime and they weren't going to let her forget it. She stooped to pet Indigo and picked up Rowena. Going to the window, she looked out on the seascape.

It was almost a full moon tonight, and the waves were exquisite shades of dark blues and grays. The incessant, steady rhythm of the waves being called by the moon to come ashore, then retreat, soothed her after the rough night. She cuddled Rowena close and rested her cheek against the white cat's fur. She heard the lop-eared Binky shuffling about in his pen.

Libby liked it here, far from anyone, alone with her animals and her music in this small cabin. She had enough interaction with people in the course of her performances. Funny, she mused. They had always assumed Harry was going to be the famous musician of the two of them. Libby's interest in the Ktarian version of the harp, the *lal-shak,* was regarded by everyone, including herself, as nothing more than a pleasant hobby.

But when Harry had gone, vanished as if swallowed, she had turned to the instrument for comfort in assuaging her grief. She had played for hours on end, played until her fingers bled, stained the fine rose-colored wood with her tears. An immense talent had come to the surface with the force of a volcano, a talent that no one, not even she, had guessed she possessed. Now she was widely regarded as the finest non-Ktarian player of the instrument in existence, and she was sought after hungrily for her musical gifts.

She was appreciated for talents other than musical as well.

Absently, she put some food into a dish for the cats, dropped some veggies and special pellets into the pen for Binky, and went into the bedroom of the small cabin.

She stood beside the bed, pressed the wall in just the right spot, and the holographic illusion of a driftwood-gray wall disappeared. In its place were a racing series of blinking lights and a control panel that put that of most starships to shame.

Libby was tired. She wanted nothing more than to fall into bed and let the ceaseless song of the ocean lull her into dreamless sleep. But she was a professional, and professionals didn't shirk their duty, no matter how tired and heartsore they might be.

She stepped forward and submitted to the retinal scan and the DNA check. The face of an attractive, pale woman with blond hair appeared on the screen.

"Agent Webber," said Brenna Covington, director of Starfleet Intelligence's Covert Operations. "I've been waiting for your report."

Chapter

5

IT WAS ONLY THE SECOND TIME Libby had laid eyes on the director. Brenna Covington was notorious for keeping to herself, even for someone in charge of Covert Operations and Deep Cover assignments, Earth Division. She met with agents on a "need to know" basis. Libby had been doing well in the agency and, during her studies on Ktar, had helped to uncover a plot to attack the Federation. It was not, as everyone had first thought, a Ktarian scheme, but the plan of another alien race. Libby had helped clear the people whose music brought her such pleasure, and it had been quite a feather in her cap. She was moving steadily and swiftly through the ranks, very quickly for such a junior agent. After all, she had been with Starfleet Intelligence for only six and a half years.

Until that time, she had known only what other civilians knew about SI, which was little more than that it existed and that it helped the Federation protect itself. At that point, her whole life lay before her, and she was determined to live in the open, in the sunlight, in the light of her love's adoration. Then Harry had gone, and with his absence came a darkness in her soul that was terrifying. In her grief, she had sought knowledge of what had happened to Harry, and in a confused, jumbled way had come to the conclusion that joining Starfleet Intelligence could help her find that knowledge.

Of course, it hadn't, but in the end, it had been a good pairing. SI liked that Libby seemed an unlikely suspect, a civilian with no formal Starfleet connections. They liked that she was deceptively open-faced and appeared to be focused only on her love of performing. They liked that she was physically and personally attractive. They liked that her concerts took her all over the quadrant, for music was a universal language and appreciated even by those who wanted no part of the Federation.

And now, with *Voyager*'s sudden and shattering return, they liked that Libby had once been engaged to Harry Kim.

It was this that intrigued Director Covington, and it was this connection that made Libby Webber uniquely placed to do her other job—spying. When the call had come a week ago, Libby had of course gone to meet the Federation legend, and when Brenna Covington had asked her to attend the welcome-home banquet and report back, she had agreed.

"How are you handling it, Agent Webber?" Covington had inquired, leaning forward solicitously. She was a pale woman—pale eyes, pale skin, pale hair—but quite attractive, and almost motherly in her concern.

"I'm all right," Libby had replied. "A little nervous about meeting him."

"Our sources tell us that he hasn't made any permanent commitments," Covington went on. "Do you think he might be interested in resuming a relationship with you?"

"I—I really have no idea. He's been gone seven years."

"Yet he has remained unattached," Covington had pointed out. "As have you."

Understanding began to dawn. "Do you want me to pretend I'm still interested in him? Romantically?"

"Would it be pretending?"

Libby said nothing.

Covington leaned forward. "I'm not asking you to do this on a whim, Agent Webber. I have information that leads me to believe that we need someone on the inside with *Voyager*'s crew. It would take a long time for us to find someone else with your convenient connection. It would be well worth your while," she added.

Knowing that she was putting her career at risk, Libby had said stubbornly, "I don't think it's right to play with Harry's feelings like that."

Covington sighed. "I didn't want to tell you this, but I see I have to. The situation is grim, Agent Webber. We've got a mole."

"What?" Libby was shocked.

Covington nodded her fair head, looking somber. "There's been a great deal of technological information leaked to the Orion Syndicate. We have reason to believe that the arrival of *Voyager,* with its astonishing new technological developments, is going to be very appealing to the mole. He or she is going to want to get close to it, and the people who were on it. It's a rare chance for us to flush the mole out into the open. Considering the nature of what's been leaked, we're going on the assumption that the mole is very highly placed in Starfleet."

"Do you have a suspect?"

Covington shook her head. "No one suspect, although we've got our eye on several. None of them is below the rank of admiral. And frankly, the only ones we can rule out with certainty are the *Voyager* crew itself. It's hard to negotiate deals with the Syndicate when you're several thousand light-years away."

"But," Libby had said, puzzled, "if Harry's not under suspicion, why do you need me to . . . to be close to him?"

"Your fame as a concert performer has opened many doors," Covington replied. "You think Aidan Fletcher's commendation for the job on Ktar didn't cross my desk? If you resume an intimate relationship with Ensign Kim, you'll be able to accompany him to all kinds of functions. Quite possibly even on board *Voyager.* You'll be moving in the same elite circles we think the mole moves in. And it'll be a completely logical place for you to be."

Libby felt sick inside. She almost wished that she was entirely over Harry. It would be easier to completely fabricate an affection she didn't feel than to take her already confused emotions and point them in a specific direction.

But Brenna Covington was awaiting her reply, and both of them knew what it would be.

"I think it went as well as could be expected," Libby told Covington on the viewscreen, shaking off the memory of their first encounter. "It's hard to get very personal in a crowded banquet hall."

"But he believed you were interested in resuming your relationship?"

"Yes." Libby, too, believed she was interested in resuming the relationship. She might have exaggerated a few things here and there when speaking with Harry, but not much, not much at all. The old feelings were still surprisingly strong, even after seven years. "It was difficult to speak with any of the admirals present. Harry and his parents pretty much demanded my full attention, and to leave them would have been too conspicuous."

"That's fine, Agent Webber. Cement the relationship first and you can worry about analyzing admirals' behavior at the next function. You did very well. To be honest, I wasn't sure you'd go through with it."

Libby squared her shoulders. She needed to be truthful with this woman. "Director, I have to say that it wasn't just a great acting job tonight. I really *do* still care for Harry, and I think the closer we get, the less objective I'm going to be."

To her surprise, Covington smiled warmly. "Agent Webber, that's just fine. Harry's not the one in trouble. This can be as real a love affair as you want to make it. Starfleet Intelligence isn't going to run your life for you. Lieutenant Kim will give you the access you need, and that's all we want."

Libby relaxed slightly. "Thank you, Director. That's good to know."

"Despite what you may hear," said Covington, smiling mischievously, "I'm not an ice queen." She winked. "I do hope all goes well. Good night, Agent Webber."

"Good night, ma'am."

The screen went dark. Libby pressed the proper buttons and the holographic concealing panel rematerialized. She leaned back on the bed, her thoughts racing.

Oh, Harry. What are we going to do? What if it doesn't work? I'll hate myself for playing on your emotions.

She rose, performed her nightly ablutions, slipped into a pair of oversized, comfortable pajamas, and got into bed. One thing she knew for sure: If it didn't work out, she'd break things off the minute the assignment was done and the mole captured. Harry deserved better than to just be used, even for a good cause.

She drifted into sleep, and was haunted by dreams.

B'Elanna swallowed hard. Standing silently behind her, her husband, who knew every one of her volatile, complex moods, touched her shoulder gently with one hand. In the other arm he cradled a sleeping Miral.

The banquet was over, and B'Elanna was glad. It had been a strained, tense affair. First the uncomfortable reunion with her father, then the perfunctory awards ceremony. She didn't give a damn about her own promotion, but she was smarting on behalf of Tom, Harry, Vorik, Campbell, and especially Captain Janeway. They all deserved much more than being an add-on to a lousy banquet. Just handing out those pips as if they were party favors belittled the achievements of her hardworking fellow crewmen. It rankled and she was hardly able to eat a bite. Now they were alone in their room in the Parises' household, and she had one more task to complete before turning in and putting an end to this stressful day.

Torres took a deep breath. "Computer," she said, "put me through to Commander Logt."

In a heartbeat, Logt's strong, attractive visage appeared. "B'Elanna Torres," she said. "You received my message, then."

"I did," Torres replied, "but I'm still confused. You said that we needed to talk about my mother, and that it is a matter of some urgency. What happened to her?"

"First," Logt said, "how much do you know about your mother's recent activities?"

Tired, nerves strained to the breaking point, B'Elanna snapped, "How the hell should I know anything? I've been lost in the Delta Quadrant for seven years!"

Logt's eyes flashed; then she opened a mouth full of sharp, jagged teeth and laughed. "So you are a Klingon after all! I was beginning to have my doubts. And you are right. I should have realized you would know nothing."

Although the commander had conceded that Torres's point was valid, somehow B'Elanna felt as though she'd just been insulted. Tom's hand gently squeezed her shoulder and she bit back the angry retort. She took a deep breath and said, "I have only just returned. Please. Tell me about my mother."

"She came here to Boreth about a year after your ship had been deemed lost," said Logt.

"Boreth?" Torres was confused. "It's a spiritual community, not a military outpost. What is a commander doing there?"

Logt sat up straighter, and for the first time Torres noticed the baldric that draped from her right shoulder to the left side of the waist. It was red and gold. This was one of the emperor's personal guards.

"His Excellency Kahless wished a small military presence here," Logt said. "It is a high honor indeed."

Torres was certain it was, but she was also equally certain that it annoyed a military officer no end to be stationed in such a peaceful place. She hoped Logt wasn't chafing under the "honor." Even though she had distanced herself from all things Klingon, B'Elanna remembered well the commotion that Kahless's return had caused. The clone created by the priests of Boreth was not the mighty warrior returned from the dead, that much was true. But apparently he had Kahless's wisdom and dignity, and would hold the seat of emperor until the real Kahless returned to claim it. Of course he'd have an honor guard stationed at the most holy site in his empire.

"I should have recognized your position," Torres said. "Please continue."

Logt nodded, accepting the compliment graciously. "Miral wished to immerse herself in honoring Kahless, to petition him to bring her daughter safely home. She was a supplicant, as all are supplicants, but at one point she fell into a deep dream state. She awoke having had a vision of you, B'Elanna. She did not share the details, but she was determined to honor Kahless for the vision and went on the Challenge of Spirit."

A little ashamed of her ignorance, Torres said, "I'm not familiar with that."

"You chose a human life," said Logt, clearly trying not to sound contemptuous but largely failing. "You might be more familiar with the human term 'vision quest.' "

Torres nodded. "I do know that term," she said. "One goes out into the wilderness and scorns food and water, seeking an altered state in order to receive a vision."

"It is a bit more with us," Logt said. "One pushes oneself to the limit of physical endurance. One uses ancient techniques to make weapons to slay one's food and fend off attacks, to make clothing and find shelter. It is a true test of the Klingon spirit. To endure so for a few months bestows great honor. To last a full year in the wild, with only one's wits and courage, is worthy of a great ceremony."

A sinking feeling came over B'Elanna. "My mother . . . she never returned, did she?"

The harsh visage softened. "No," Logt said, quietly. "She did not."

Torres swallowed hard. She remembered every moment of her own vision of the Barge of the Dead. She hadn't been sure what to call it—a dream, a hallucination, an active imagination working overtime. Now she felt the first tremblings of true belief. Her mother had had a vision of connecting with her at about the same time as B'Elanna's own experience. She knew what Chakotay would say: Mother and daughter had shared a vision. Could it be possible? Was this more than a coincidence? Torres had never thought of herself as mystical and had in fact had to bite her tongue whenever Chakotay waxed eloquent about his personal spirituality. The one time she'd attempted to enter his world, she had tried to kill her animal guide. No, the ethereal realms of mystery and magic were not anywhere B'Elanna Torres had been inclined to travel.

But now . . . .

She had clung to the final words spoken by her mother: *In* Sto-Vo-Kor *. . . or maybe . . . when you get home.* She blinked back quick tears. It would seem that *Sto-Vo-Kor,* after all, would be the only place she would see her mother again.

She felt Tom's hand still warm on her shoulder. She was so grateful for him, for little Miral. Torres cleared her throat.

"I am thankful that you felt telling me my mother's fate so important," she said. "But I am confused. I don't see how it's urgent."

"Our tradition dictates that if a seeker is deemed lost on the Challenge of Spirit, her earthly possessions are to be destroyed within a certain time after the seeker is declared lost to *Sto-Vo-Kor.* That time is rapidly approaching. I thought perhaps you would wish to claim what she left with us before it is hurled into the ritual fire of cleansing."

"Oh, yes," said Torres. She didn't care what it was, clothing, toiletries, even the most mundane items would have meaning for her. "Yes, I would."

"Then you need to be here in five days at the most," said Logt.

"Five days— I can't possibly—"

"B'Elanna," said Tom, speaking quietly into her ear, "my father can pull some strings if he needs to."

"And His Excellency has offered to see to it that you reach Boreth in time," said Logt, startling both Tom and B'Elanna.

"Kahless cares about what happens to my mother's stuff?"

"He does. Miral sought an audience with him before she left on her Challenge, to share her vision with him. Apparently, he was quite impressed. A vessel is standing by at this moment to take you to Boreth."

"Give me a half hour," said Torres.

"I will meet you at the holy site upon your arrival, " said Logt. She pressed a button and the transmission ended.

"Wow," said Tom. "That doesn't give us very long to get ready."

B'Elanna turned in her chair to look up at her husband and daughter. She extended a finger and ran it gently along the protruding ridges along Miral's oh-so-Klingon forehead. She was so glad now that the Doctor had prevented her from changing a single thing. Her daughter was beautiful, perfect. A fierce tide of love swept through her, both for the infant and the man who had sired her.

"Thank you for coming with me," she said. "I would have hated to have to leave you so soon."

"Hey," said Tom, gently, "you don't get rid of this cute little bundle of responsibility that easily, you know. Or Miral either," he added, jokingly.

She smiled, then sobered. "It could take a while," she

said. "Who knows what kind of ritual they'll make me do. They may not even let non-Klingons on the planet."

"I've got nothing but free time until I'm reassigned, and all Miral has to do is grow and be healthy and loved. You just make sure we've got nice quarters on that ship and we'll be fine." He touched her cheek. "Take all the time you need. We're not going anywhere."

She knew he knew how much his words meant to her, and she felt a lump in her throat as she reached one hand out to her husband, the other to her sleeping child.

Chapter

6

JANEWAY STOOD LOOKING around at her austere, clean apartment. She was partly amused, partly despairing. This new place was waiting for her in San Francisco, courtesy of Starfleet Command. All the senior staff had been offered that option. Some had declined, others accepted. For the moment, Janeway had said yes, and was now doing her best to decorate it with the furniture and knickknacks her mother had recovered when she had been given up for lost. They had stayed in the attic in the house in Indiana, and now they looked rumpled and pitiful in the gleaming Starfleet-provided apartment. Janeway sighed. The banquet had run late—no one had wanted to leave, to really say good-bye—and she knew she ought to be getting to bed.

The door chimed. "Come," she said, surprised—who

knew she was here, and who would call at this hour?— and turned to greet her first visitor.

The door hissed open, and Mark Johnson stood there. For a moment, she didn't breathe. "Hello, Kathryn," he said gently. "I hope it was all right for me to come. I spoke with your mother and she seemed to think so."

"Mark," she said, recovering. "Yes, of course. It's so good to see you."

He held out his arms and she went to him. Even as she laid her head on his chest, she saw the light wink against the simple gold band on his left finger. She knew he'd gotten married, and oddly, she felt no pain at the thought. Only pleasure that he had found someone, again, to love. He was a good and gentle man, and deserved it.

"I'm so glad you're home," he said, his breath on her hair. They pulled apart, and Janeway saw that his eyes, too, were filled with tears.

"Thank you for coming," she said, stepping away. "Can I make you some coffee?" she asked, and then had a brief moment of distress when she realized that she didn't know where the replicator was in this new place.

"No, thanks. Hang on—I've got something of yours I need to return to you."

While he was gone, Janeway took the opportunity to recover. She hadn't realized how much she had missed him. More correctly, she hadn't *let* herself realize how much she had missed him. But now, seeing him after all this time, feeling him warm and strong against her—

"Stop it, Kathryn," she told herself in a low voice. "No sense wasting energy on could-have-beens." And yet, it was difficult.

A dog's bark shattered her thoughts and she turned. Sitting beside Mark in the front room, a little heavier than she remembered and graying around the muzzle, was Molly.

"Oh, Molly!" she called, kneeling and opening her arms to the animal. Molly looked up uncertainly at Mark, then back at Janeway. The Irish setter tilted her head quizzically.

Janeway forced a smile through the pain. Of course Molly wouldn't remember her. It had been seven years. She straightened and laughed uncomfortably.

"That was a little foolish, I suppose," she said. "You've been her master for most of her life."

Mark smiled his easy, comfortable smile. "Hey, I've only been dog-sitting. She's always been yours. I can tell you who took the puppies, if you'd like to know. Everyone was so excited about your return. They feel like they own a celebrity dog. They'd be honored if you'd visit."

"Maybe I will," she said, though in truth, she thought she probably wouldn't. She didn't know those dogs, those people. So much had changed. "Keep her, Mark. You've loved her and taken care of her for seven years. She's your dog, now."

He seemed about to argue, then took a long look at her and nodded. That, at least, hadn't changed. He knew her so well. He always had been able to see through her bravado. It was that quality that had made her fall in love with him in the first place.

She sat on the couch that clashed horribly with the surroundings and indicated that he do likewise. Molly, relaxed and calm, began to sniff Janeway's still-packed things.

They sat, stiffly. There were only a few inches of distance between them, but it might as well have been kilometers. Neither spoke for a while.

Finally, Mark broke the uncomfortable silence. "Kathryn, this is awkward. For both of us. You know that if I believed you were alive and coming home, I'd have waited."

"Of course I do," she said swiftly. "You did nothing wrong, Mark. I'd have done the same thing."

He looked haunted. "Would you? I wonder. It's just— Kathryn, we were friends long before we were anything else. I have always admired and respected you, and that hasn't changed. If anything, it's grown. You're . . . amazing to me. I think about you every day. Carla understands how important a person you were in my life. I'd like for you to continue to be in my life as it is now, with Carla and Kevin."

"Kevin?"

"Our son." He laughed. "He's a petty tyrant, but we love him. I'd like for him to get to know his Aunt Kathryn." His eyes were somber. "Will he?"

There was no question in her mind, only happiness. She extended her left hand. He took it, squeezed it. "Of course," she said. "I wouldn't miss being a part of that for the universe, Mark."

And for the first time since he'd walked back into her life, the ghost and shadows around his eyes lifted, and he smiled from his heart.

* * *

She had dinner with the Johnsons the following night, and after a few strained minutes, Janeway found herself feeling right at home. The toddler Kevin was indeed a petty tyrant, but all was forgiven when he smiled. Not even Naomi Wildman had been so cute at that tender age.

Mark's wife Carla was a lovely woman. She was a little younger than Janeway or Mark, with a sharp brain, a cheerful grin, and an easy manner that Janeway responded to immediately. Molly was obviously well loved and looked after, and as the evening progressed she seemed to remember Janeway a little bit more. It felt good.

A brief crisis came when Carla, who had tried to actually bake a soufflé, yelped in the kitchen. She stuck her head out. "Mark, Kathryn . . . I'm so sorry. The dessert is a total disaster. I should have replicated it. I'm sorry," she repeated.

"Carla, it's all right. I'm so full from your delicious dinner that I probably wouldn't have done it justice anyway," Janeway said. It was no lie; her stomach was straining.

Carla seemed unduly distressed by the fallen soufflé. Janeway sensed it was more than just a failed dessert. Mark suggested that they take coffee outside. It was a balmy summer evening, and the Johnsons lived in the country. Janeway eased back in her chair and inhaled the redolent scents of roses and grass. Mark had gone in to get them each a second cup of coffee, and Carla took the opportunity to be blunt.

"I was quite jealous, you know," she said, cutting to the chase.

Janeway looked over at the younger woman. "Really?"

She nodded her head earnestly. "Really. It was always Kathryn this, Kathryn that. He had such a great relationship with you that it was like you were always present, even when it was just the two of us."

Janeway put her elbows on the table and regarded the young woman intently. "I'm no threat to you, Carla."

"Oh!" Carla's eyes flew wide. "Oh, Kathryn, no, that's not what I meant! I meant that you seemed like such a wonderful person that I was jealous of Mark for having been so close to you. I wished I'd known you, too. I wished I'd had a Kathryn Janeway to go to with all my problems. And now—well, look at you! You're a hero, and my house is a mess and my soufflé fell!"

No wonder Mark had fallen in love with this beautiful woman. What a generous spirit she had. On impulse, Janeway rose and embraced her. Carla enthusiastically returned the hug. Mark returned with two steaming mugs of coffee and grinned at the sight.

"You're a lucky man, Mark Johnson," said Janeway, pulling apart a little way from Carla. The younger woman's eyes shone with pleasure.

"Yes," he said, looking from one of them to the other. "Yes, I certainly am."

She hadn't wanted to leave, and it was clear that Mark and Carla didn't want her to, either. They even offered her the guest bedroom as the night grew late and threw in a tempting offer of homemade waffles for breakfast, but she declined. When she transported out, to rematerialize in the strange, unfamiliar apartment, Janeway wished she had accepted their generous invitation. Tonight, with Mark and her new, wonderful friend Carla, was the first time she felt really "at home."

As she puttered about, delaying getting into the strange bed, she realized what it was that made her so reluctant to claim this space as her own. She missed *Voyager*. She missed the sounds of the vessel, the feel of the chairs and the bed, the wide starfield that she would often gaze at for a long time before finally drifting off into a restless sleep.

It was late, almost two in the morning. Yet, she sat down and tapped the small viewscreen on the table. The sound would be soft, she knew. If he didn't want to answer, he wouldn't have to. No insistent combadges, not anymore.

His face appeared on the screen. Like her, he was fully dressed and seemed wide awake. "Hi," he said, smiling.

"Hi," she said feeling her own lips stretch into a grin.

"Couldn't sleep?" asked Chakotay.

"Nope."

"Funny, me neither."

"Too quiet. No Borg attacks at all."

"Know what you mean. And no starfields to go to sleep by."

She shook her head.

"Want to come over for some coffee?" he asked.

"The real stuff?"

"But of course. That's half the reason we came home, isn't it?" His smile faded slightly.

"What is it?" Janeway asked. Over the last seven years, she had learn to recognize every expression that flitted over that dark, handsome face.

"I'm planning on taking a trip shortly," he said. "A

very important one. I was wondering if you'd like to accompany me."

Seven felt awkward sitting doing nothing in the shuttle. She was more used to piloting them than being a passenger in them, and the nervousness the young ensign displayed only added to her discomfort.

Nearly everyone else aboard *Voyager* had some relative or friend they were staying with who had been at the banquet. The only contact Seven had was her Aunt Irene, who was ill and unable to attend. When Admiral Paris had learned of this, he had made a gallant show of having one of his protégés formally escort her to her aunt's home in the country. Seven protested, saying that she could simply use a transporter. Paris would have none of that. And when Chakotay offered her a lift instead, Seven had decided to accept Admiral Paris's offer. Now she wasn't so certain.

"It really is an honor to be the one selected to escort you home, ma'am," said the youth. His voice didn't quite break, but he was certainly more a boy than a man.

"That is the third time you have said so, Ensign Randolph," said Seven. She regretted her words as the young man's face flushed bright red. Even his ears were red.

"I'm sorry if I offended you," she said genuinely. "I'm not used to being . . . idolized. It is not a comfortable sensation."

Randolph turned to look at her, his blue eyes shining. "Oh, but ma'am, you've been with the Borg most of your life, and yet you were able to walk away from their evil without a second look back."

"Hardly true," said Seven. "There was a long time indeed where I wanted nothing more than to return to the collective. It was only Captain—Admiral Janeway's faith in me that kept me among the ranks of humans."

He looked puzzled. A little of her allure had no doubt just been removed as far as he was concerned. Seven was glad of it. The sooner people stopped thinking she was some kind of goddess, the better she—

"What is that?" she said, looking at a small sea of colors as they began their descent. Quickly, she was able to answer her own question as they drew closer.

Dozens of people had formed a ring around her aunt's house. A huge banner sported the words BYE-BYE BORG, HELLO SEVEN OF NINE! There was a hot-air balloon hovering close to the shuttle.

"Geez," said Randolph. "Oh, geez." He looked a little panicky as he thumbed the controls. "Ensign Randolph to Admiral Paris. We have a heck of a welcome-home party here for Miss Seven. What would you like me to do?"

"Damn," said Paris, and to his credit he sounded rueful. "Someone must have leaked Irene Hansen's address. Seven, I'm sorry, but you're just going to have to run the gauntlet here. Randolph, I authorize you to use force if the crowd becomes too much for you to handle."

"It's just a welcome-home party, sir. I doubt they'll become violent."

But Seven was staring at the huge crush of people, and her breathing grew rapid and shallow. So many of them. She was used to being with hundreds of drones at a time, of course. She had experienced more years of other voices in her head, other beings at her side, than she had years of being alone. But these weren't Borg drones, comfortable and familiar in their predictability. These were individuals. Without data, their behavior could not be at all predicted, and that made her nervous. She had thought the people who had gathered around her at the banquet had been bad enough, but that had only been about twenty or thirty people at the most. She was looking now at dozens, perhaps hundreds.

My arrival here is not a spectator sport! Anger surged through her. She had done nothing to these people. Why were they denying her a quiet, calm reunion with her aunt?

"We should return," she stated. "They will disperse once they see I am not disembarking."

Randolph laughed. "Ma'am, I'm willing to bet some of these people have been camping out here for days, ever since news of *Voyager*'s arrival was made public. They know you're going to have to disembark sometime."

"I will transport in."

"I don't think you quite grasp the level of your celebrity, ma'am. Certainly you can transport directly into your aunt's living room, but this crowd isn't going to go away until they lay eyes on you in person. It's you they want."

Seven's eyes narrowed. "Then I shall give myself to them," she said. Something about her tone of voice made Randolph look at her uneasily, but he did not comment.

"Shall I take her down then, ma'am?"

"Proceed, Ensign."

The nearest place to land the shuttle was several yards from the old farmhouse that Irene Hansen called home. Randolph made straight for it, and Seven watched with revulsion as the tiny figures raced toward the clearing where the shuttle would set down. Ants. They looked like ants, racing along with a sense of purpose that ironically turned them into mindless beings.

Randolph landed the shuttle with great skill, considering the circumstances. He turned to her and started to say, "Let me go out first and—" But it was too late. Seven had already opened the door and jumped lightly to the grass.

A cheer rose up. Seven saw the handmade banners waving, saw the horde of people literally running to her. She stood her ground and tapped a small device on her chest, similar to the communicator she had worn every day on *Voyager.* The adjustment would magnify her voice.

"Attention!" Seven cried. "I am not here to converse with any of you. Not the press. Not curious onlookers with nothing better to do. Not any of you who claim to be long-lost friends of my parents. Not those of you who have subjected your children to this barbaric gathering in order to let them supposedly have a glimpse of history. I am not your plaything. I don't belong to you, and neither does my aunt. You are on private property. You will leave this place at once and not return. If you do not comply, I will order this ensign to fire into the crowd with a phaser set on stun. Am I understood?"

Without waiting for a reaction, she strode through

the crowd. It didn't part for her, and she heard the happy cheers mutate into outraged, wordless cries of insult and anger. She pushed. They pushed back. Before she knew what was happening, she was trapped in a tight circle of strangers. Their faces were furious, and they were yelling things at her, grabbing at her. She steeled herself to fight back. She was stronger than anyone here, and she could—

There was the sharp whine of a phaser. One of the biggest men pawing at Seven collapsed.

"Everyone, please!" Randolph's voice was high, but his young face was resolute. "Seven of Nine has undergone a great deal. I'm certain she didn't mean to sound so harsh, but she is exhausted and unused to this kind of attention. Please let her return to her home. I have no wish to set this phaser on wide-range. Let Seven alone."

They backed away from her, but not far. She heard the taunts and jeers as she strode as swiftly as she could toward the beckoning of her aunt's front porch.

"Didn't get your heart back when they made you human, huh?"

"Think you're better than us?"

"You were my hero!"

"We thought you were human again, but you're still a Borg!"

Her heart was pounding rapidly in her chest and her neck hurt from holding her head so high. She wanted to break into a run but would not give them the satisfaction. Seven tuned out the scathing words shouted by the crowd and then, at last, her feet touched the wooden steps of her aunt's porch. She ran up them, unable to control herself, opened the door, and escaped inside.

"Oh, this is just great," said Randolph, who had barely made it in behind Seven before she slammed the door shut and leaned against it. "I don't think I've ever seen anyone alienate a crowd quicker in my life."

The hero worship that had shone in his eyes was gone. He now looked merely annoyed and a little frightened of the people outside.

"They had no right to be here," Seven said, a touch defensively. "This is private property. Is it so much to ask that I be allowed to greet my aunt without a swarm of people demanding my attention?"

Randolph sighed. "You just don't get it, Seven." No more "ma'am," Seven noticed. "You're a celebrity, a hero. You're a Borg who was liberated from the collective—a symbol of humanity's triumph over the worst enemy we've ever encountered. All you needed to do was say a few polite words, smile and wave, and they'd have gone home happy."

"You are just like your parents," came an elderly woman's voice. Irene Hansen was slowly coming down the stairs. She clutched the railing, but was moving under her own power. "Iconoclasts, both of them. More interested in ruffling feathers than smoothing them, I'm afraid. That's not the Borg in her irritating those people outside, young man. That's her mother and father."

A wave of pleasure rushed over Seven, along with a sense of awkwardness. "Aunt Irene," she said, her voice sounding stiff and formal in her own ears. "Are you well enough to be walking?"

"I'm over the worst of it," Irene said. "You come here and give me a hug."

Even as she heard Randolph speaking to Paris, with words like "situation here" and "could use some security" and "need to issue a statement" sprinkled in his conversation, Seven moved quickly toward her aunt. Irene stood on the last step, her arms extended, her wrinkled face alight. Seven extended her own arms and enfolded the older woman in a tight embrace. She smelled a pleasant floral scent, felt the odd combination of fragility and strength in Irene's body, and wondered if her parents would have felt this way in her arms. The thought made tears come to her eyes.

"Annika," said Irene. "Sweet, sweet child. Welcome home."

Three days after the welcome-home banquet, Tuvok materialized in the front hall of his own home. The colors were slightly different. He took a moment to note the changes his wife had made in his absence. Instead of the muted, dark purple hues he remembered, there were now shades of blue and green. The ancient urn that had stood in the hallway alcove had been moved to the top of the stairs. It had been replaced by a landscape painting of the Voroth Sea. It was quite striking. Looking closer, he saw that it bore the name of his youngest child, T'Pev. He raised an eyebrow. T'Pev had always had an eye for fine art, and it was good to see that the child had not squandered her talents.

"They told us that you did not wish us to travel to

Earth to greet you, once Sek had completed the *fal-tor-voh*," a soft, female voice said.

Despite himself, despite his years of discipline, Tuvok could not suppress a quickening of his pulse. He did not permit himself to turn around immediately.

"That is correct," he said, keeping his voice modulated. "There was no logic in disrupting the present status of your lives for an excessive and unnecessary human-inspired celebration. Once I was cured, I would then be debriefed and able to return to Vulcan shortly thereafter."

"I agree, husband," said T'Pel, stepping into the light as he turned around. "There was no reason to rush this reunion. I have waited seven years for your safe return. A few days more is insignificant. I trust that the *fal-tor-voh* was successful?"

"Entirely. Sek is a worthy son and performed the mind-meld admirably."

He moved toward her. They were only inches apart now. Her shining brown eyes, tranquil as a pool on temple grounds, met his evenly. Slowly, Tuvok lifted his right hand and extended the first two fingers. T'Pel hesitated, and then lifted her own hand. Their fingers touched.

He did not wish it, but something stirred within him. Tuvok was still recovering from the effects of the recently cured neurological dysfunction. The mind-meld with Sek had been a balm to an injury. Peace had descended upon Tuvok's restless, churning mind once more as his son reached and touched his mind, calmly eradicating all hints of the degeneration.

A faint frown rippled across T'Pel's smooth, lovely

face as she sensed the agony and confusion he had undergone . . . and something more. Something that was, no doubt, directly caused by the lingering effects of the condition.

"On the other hand," T'Pel continued smoothly, "it is also illogical to behave as if you had not been gone for so long a time, is it not?"

"Most illogical," he agreed. Her flesh was warm against his, her mind open to him through the intimate touch of finger against finger.

Although he had, most inconveniently, undergone *Pon farr* very recently aboard *Voyager,* where the primal desires thus roused were slaked by a holographic version of the female now standing before him, Tuvok experienced an echo of that powerful desire. Sensing his thoughts, T'Pel lifted an eyebrow in inquiry.

There was no need for words. As he accompanied his wife to their bedchamber, Tuvok reflected on how, under certain extreme circumstances, the descent of *Pon farr* was not always required to elicit the mating response.

Chapter
7

THE FORMER FIRST OFFICER AND CAPTAIN of the *U.S.S. Voyager* had enjoyed the past few days they'd spent together, although Chakotay refused to reveal their destination.

The ship that he jokingly called the "Alpha Flyer" zipped along with a smoothness that belied its rough exterior. Janeway relaxed and leaned back in the copilot's seat of the little craft.

"Nice ship, Captain Chakotay," she said. He threw her a quick grin.

"Always told you I wanted a nice little ship of my own," he said. "You know, as a first officer, you're not half bad."

"Coming from the best first officer it's been my pleasure to know, I'm flattered." "You know, Tom Paris would call this a 'road trip,'" she added.

"I like this better than a Camaro," Chakotay replied.

The stars streaked by as they sat in comfortable silence for a while. Finally, Janeway said, "I understand that all the former Maquis on *Voyager* were offered the opportunity to return to Starfleet, with all rank returned."

"It was a generous offer," said Chakotay, reaching down and tapping the console.

"Will it be one you accept?"

"I don't know yet." He turned to look at her, and his dark eyes were serious. "I hadn't expected our return to be without its difficulties, but I confess, I'm surprised at some of the emotions it's stirring up."

"I know exactly what you mean," said Janeway, thinking of Mark, Carla, and little Kevin. "I don't think we realized just how sheltered we were on *Voyager*."

"I had a chance to meet with Sveta and some of the other Maquis at the banquet. For them, it's all the past, but for me—well, not having been there, not having gone through it with them, it's still pretty raw."

Even at their most intimate over the last seven years, Chakotay had never spoken quite so freely. Janeway was touched by his confidence. She had thought they had grown close, and was certain that they had, but clearly, that barrier between captain and crewman had blocked off more than she had thought.

"Speaking of the banquet," she said, "and feel free to tell me to mind my own business if you'd like, but I noticed that you and Seven weren't sitting together."

His face was impassive. "Seven feels that while our

relationship might have flourished had we stayed on *Voyager,* it won't now that we've reached Earth. She needs to find out who she is here, and I agreed. Hell, *I* need to find out who I am here."

Janeway nodded her comprehension. She thought so. Much as Seven liked to think of herself as cool and collected, her emotions were an easy book to read to anyone who knew and loved her. She was sorry for Chakotay, but not surprised.

She took a look at the coordinates of their destination. Somehow, it seemed familiar. Then Janeway realized where they were headed, and her stomach tightened. Chakotay was bringing her along with him to face some of the demons of his past.

They did not speak the rest of the time, but sat, each lost in private thoughts. Finally, Chakotay dropped out of warp and into orbit around a small moon. He leaned back, took a deep breath, and exhaled slowly through his mouth. Janeway recognized it for what it was: a calming breath, to steady himself for what lay ahead.

He straightened, resumed control, and took the *Alpha Flyer* down. Tom Paris couldn't have made a smoother landing, and when he set them down gently, Janeway looked out at the deceptive beauty of this moon that housed such a horror.

They got out and walked toward a tall standing stone. On it was a bronze plaque. "I didn't know Starfleet had marked this already," Janeway said, her voice hushed and reverent as if she were in a holy place. In a very real sense, she was.

"They haven't," Chakotay replied, his own voice

soft. "Sveta and some of the other Maquis did this all on their own."

Strangely, Janeway felt stung by the comment. "I'm certain Starfleet would have gotten around to making this official," she said.

"I'm not. There's a lot on their minds right now. Memorializing people once considered traitors can't be very high on their list."

The plaque read:

On this site, on Stardate 50953.4, one of the most brutal massacres of the Dominion War took place. For many months, Tevlik's moon had been a secret base for the group calling themselves the Maquis, who fought a private war based on their highest morals and ethics against the Cardassians, whom they regarded as the enemy. It was considered a safe place, and many brought their families here to protect them from repercussions. Due to the betrayal of one of their leaders, a Bajoran called Arak Katal, the entire population of the base was wiped out by a surprise Cardassian attack.

Four thousand two hundred fifty-six men, women, and children were slaughtered. The Cardassians took no prisoners. This plaque is to commemorate the dead. May they never be forgotten, and may the principles for which they stood always be remembered.

There followed a list of names, many that Janeway recognized. She'd been told about the attack, of course, but she hadn't realized there had been whole Maquis families based here. Nor had she fully appreciated the sheer number of lives lost. And she had not known that they were betrayed by one of their own. For a moment, she and Chakotay stood in reverent silence.

Finally Janeway said softly, "What became of Arak?"

"No one knows," answered Chakotay. "He could have been a Cardassian agent, like Seska. Or he could have had other reasons for betraying us. According to Sveta, he simply disappeared. He had better never show his face in this quadrant," he added, his voice suddenly harsh and angry. "I know many who'd kill him on sight. I'd be one of them."

"With B'Elanna right behind you," said Janeway. "I hope it doesn't come to that. I'd hate to have to visit you in prison for the rest of your life."

He looked at her and smiled, a little. There was no hint that there had been a base here. All equipment had been salvaged long ago; all the dead, identified and buried. All that remained was this standing stone and the plaque.

"Will we ever move beyond this?" Janeway suddenly said, the words bursting from her. "We claim to be so advanced, to value peace and good relationships with all species. And yet, I stand here, and I see this, and I wonder."

"I wonder too," said Chakotay. "Peace is precious. But there is such a thing as too high a price for peace."

She reached out and slipped a comforting arm around his waist. His arm came up and draped across her shoulders. They stood like that, side by side, wordlessly thinking about peace, and prices, and other destinies.

"If I hadn't been hiding in the Badlands," said Chakotay, "I'd have been operating from this base. It's more than likely that my name would be there, too."

Janeway shuddered at the thought. "Do you feel guilty that you didn't die with them?" she asked, softly.

He didn't answer at once. Finally, he said, "No. I was where destiny placed me. I shirked nothing. But I desperately wish that Starfleet had seen what we had seen earlier, that the Cardassians were not to be trusted. Then maybe all these good people would still be alive."

Slowly, they turned and walked back to the small ship. As they lifted off, Janeway turned to Chakotay and said, "I'm glad our destinies coincided, Chakotay. It was a privilege to have you at my side these past seven years."

He smiled. "And it was a privilege to serve with you, Captain. Or I suppose I should say Admiral now."

She laughed and held up a hand in protest. "Kathryn. I'm not your captain anymore."

"Ah," he joked, "you'll always be Captain to me."

Suddenly serious, she looked into his dark eyes. "I hope not," she said.

For Tom and B'Elanna, the five-day trip to Boreth, deep in the heart of the Klingon empire, seemed to take four years. B'Elanna was only reluctantly acknowledged by the captain, who had apparently been pulled off a more important assignment to "ferry" her to Boreth, and Tom and Miral were regarded with outright contempt. There was a bad moment right at the beginning when it looked as though the two of them would be refused passage, but B'Elanna had managed to talk some sense into the captain. Well, yell some sense into him, anyway. They stayed in their cramped cabin, out of the way, until on the fifth day the captain asked Torres to report to the bridge.

"This is it," said B'Elanna. Tom gathered her into his arms and kissed her deeply.

"Don't worry about us," he said, as he gave her their child to kiss. "Old Captain Grumpyguts will leave us alone until you come back. I hope—I hope it's not too hard on you, whatever happens."

She gave him as reassuring a smile as she could manage, then went to the Klingon vessel's bridge.

"I summoned you to the bridge to see this before we transported down," said the captain of the Klingon ship to Torres. She stepped slowly down into the main area of the bridge, her eyes glued on the screen.

The Spires of Boreth. She vaguely recalled Miral waxing eloquent about their beauty. Of course, B'Elanna had ignored her mother. Surely nothing Klingon could be graceful and lovely. But B'Elanna was wrong, and as she stared at the spires catching the first morning light, turning shades of gold and rose, she understood why this place was so revered.

"Isn't there some kind of poem?" she asked. "About the spires? Something about spears to the stars."

The elderly Klingon captain nodded and quoted:

> *"Standing like spears to the stars*
> *The Spires of Boreth pierce the heavens*
> *A glorious army of spirit*
> *To be wielded at Kahless's return."*

"It's more lyrical in the original Klingon," Torres said. She took one more look at the spires, their gracefulness all the more startling in their contrast to the rough wilderness that comprised the rest of the planet, and went to the transporter room.

The first word that occurred to her as she materialized in the Great Hall of the temple was *medieval.* Seen from the ship, the spires reminded her of ancient Earth towns, and the ornate yet antiquated structure and decorations of the Great Hall further enforced that perception. Animal skins covered much of the gray stone flooring. Torches burned in sconces along the walls, and even the hanging lights were candles. A row of statues in various poses stretched along the right side of this massive corridor. She couldn't quite identify each particular one, but she assumed that they depicted scenes from the life of the great hero to whom this temple was dedicated. Paintings, too, covered the walls, paintings done in hues of angry red and shadow black.

From somewhere came a faint monotone sound, deep and rich. She assumed it was chanting. The whole place was overwhelming, intimidating. She could only guess at the power the lava caves exerted over impressionable pilgrims. The exotic atmosphere, the rituals involving fasting and steam and heat, the nearly toxic gases the lava emitted, well, it was no wonder to her that Klingons had visions with astonishing frequency here.

Her probably blasphemous thoughts were interrupted by a female's voice. "You enjoy cutting it close, B'Elanna Torres. Another hour and your mother's possessions would be leaping flame and black smoke."

Torres turned to greet Commander Logt. She was even more impressive in person than on the viewscreen. Tall, powerfully built, her dark eyes snapping with pride and confidence, she stood with her hands planted firmly on her hips. The baldric that marked her enviable position cut a vibrant swath across her body.

"It was not a question of enjoyment, but necessity," said Torres. "I got here as soon as I could."

"Come," said Logt. Without another word, she turned and strode down the hall at a brisk pace. Torres had to struggle to keep up. They went down a long, tight circular staircase for what seemed like an eternity; then it opened into another small corridor with several rooms. At the third room, Logt paused. She took a torch from a sconce and wordlessly shoved it at Torres, who took it. Logt removed a key that was as large as her hand and inserted it in the rusting metal lock.

"Why is everything so . . ." Torres struggled to find a word that would not be interpreted as offensive.

"Out of date?" said Logt, saving Torres the trouble. "All is as it was when it was first built. If anything is damaged beyond repair, Klingon artisans craft an identical replacement. Nothing here is replicated. Even the food is gathered by ritual hunting parties. It is a powerful reminder of the ancient nature of our tradition. We have one small chamber for communications with the outside universe, but that's all."

The key turned. Logt pushed, and the door groaned as it opened. The room inside was larger than Torres had expected. It was lined with row after row of shelves, from the floor to the ceiling, which was high indeed. The only light came from several small windows at the very top. Torres understood the need for the torch.

The shelves were filled with clothing, amulets, armor, weapons—all the intimate, personal belongings of those who had gone out on the Challenge of Spirit and who had never returned. There was so much, all of it deeply private. B'Elanna felt like a voyeur.

"How many are on this quest?" B'Elanna asked.

"Right now, over two thousand."

"And how many make it back?"

Logt perused her for a moment. "Fewer than a third. Boreth's wilderness is a dangerous place. Otherwise, there would be no purpose to the Challenge."

Logt unhooked a ladder from behind the door and propped it up. She climbed nimbly up several shelves, searched quickly, found what she was looking for, and swiftly descended. Without a word, she handed a neatly tied bundle to B'Elanna.

"May I . . . is there . . . ."

"Outside there is a chair. You may sit in private and examine the belongings. Keep what you wish. The rest you may leave in a pile by the door and it will be ceremonially burned."

In a pile by the door. Her mother's things. It seemed so heartless, but B'Elanna recalled how Klingons viewed a dead body. It meant nothing to them, after they had uttered the loud, piercing scream to alert those in *Sto-Vo-Kor* that a warrior was on the way to join them. Clothing and other items certainly would have no value once she who owned them had died.

"Take your time. When you are done, come back the way you came. A priest will be waiting for you and will contact your ship."

Torres nodded. "Thank you. I would have hated to have been too late."

Logt's harsh mien gentled somewhat, and she nodded once. Then, briskly, she strode down the stone corridor, the sound of her boots echoing in the stillness. B'Elanna heard her quick steps ascend, then fade into silence.

She stared at the bundle, then sat and cradled it in her lap. Taking a deep breath, she untied the complex knot and the bundle fell open.

A wooden hairbrush, its bristles thick and coarse to manage tough Klingon hair. A few strands were still entwined in them. A head covering of gold and red material shot through with black. B'Elanna supposed it was for some of the more elaborate rituals. One probably had to cover one's face or something. A robe that B'Elanna remembered from her childhood. She ran her fingers over the thick folds, recalling tugging impatiently on her mother's sleeves for something or other. A pair of slippers—odd for Klingons, who almost always wore boots. Again, probably demanded for some ritual.

And that was it. It was difficult to believe that the ferocity and passion of Miral had been reduced to a handful of clothing. Impulsively, B'Elanna decided to try on the robe. She slipped it over her head and to her surprise it fit, although a bit loosely. It was even a little short on her. Her mother had always seemed so big, so imposing. Now B'Elanna fit easily into her clothes.

She moved, and something crinkled. Puzzled, B'Elanna

reached into one of the pockets and pulled forth a small, folded piece of paper.

It was a note from Miral, reaching across the distance, the years, even from death into life. B'Elanna began to shake as she read, and by the time she was done, tears had filled her eyes. She wriggled out of the robe and folded it carelessly, trying to gather up the rest of the items quickly and dropping them as fast as she picked them up. Her fingers were nerveless, her body taut as the ancient bowstring. Finally, uttering a very Klingon grunt of annoyance, she scooped everything up into a chaotic bundle and raced for the stairs.

It was a long and demanding ascent, and by the time Torres reached the top she was gasping for breath, her heart pounding from more than simple exertion. The priest who stood by the stairs frowned terribly, but B'Elanna didn't care if she gave offense with her haste. She had a more pressing issue on her mind.

"I want to perform the Challenge of Spirit," she demanded.

AGE NINE

The girl has no friends. Her teachers are worried and send home notes expressing their concern. Her mother and the owner of the Hand attend meetings, at which they make appropriate comments and nod as if concerned. But behind the closed doors of their home, nothing changes.

The girl bears no physical signs of the damage that is wrought upon her daily. The tool she knows as a dermal regenerator closes up the lacerations, fades the bruises. The broken bones are harder to disguise. Lies flow thickly: She's so clumsy, she tripped on a toy and fell down the stairs. She's such a tomboy, always playing in the trees.

The girl keeps herself to herself. She does not raise her hand to answer questions, but frantically studies the information given and consistently makes the high-

est grades in the classroom. No one wants to play with her, and she does not invite such pastimes. No one wants to study with her. No one wants to be around her in any way, shape, or form. They do not know what they sense, these nine-year-old children, but it is as strong and as wrong as the stench of decay, and they avoid the girl completely.

She scribbles in a journal, deleting each entry once it is written lest it be discovered by the owner of the Hand. She has fantasies of coming to her instructors, of telling what the Hand does to her, to her mother, but does not dare act.

She reads the assignment dutifully, and writes her report as if her life depends upon it.

Chapter

8

"*WHAT?*"

Tom Paris seldom bellowed. He hadn't liked it when his dad had bellowed when he was younger and disliked the sound of it even more coming through his own throat. But he was bellowing now, and he knew it, and frankly he didn't give a damn.

"I know how you must feel," said B'Elanna as they stood together in their quarters on the Klingon ship. "But—"

"No," bellowed Tom, "no, you *don't* know how I feel. Damn it, B'Elanna, we've only just gotten back! Our baby is exactly two weeks old today, and you want to go on some vision quest that claims the life of one out of every three pure-blooded Klingons who attempt it?"

She bristled. "Are you saying because I'm only half-Klingon that I won't be able to make it?"

Tom sighed, his anger ebbing. Fear and frustration rushed instead to fill the void. "That's not the point and you know it."

B'Elanna made an annoyed sound and fished around in the collar of her uniform. Removing a crumpled piece of parchment, she shoved it at him.

"Read this," she snapped. Curious, he read with dawning comprehension, and nodded when he had finished. He sighed and rubbed his eyes.

"I wish you'd said this at the beginning," he said, handing the note back to her. "I hate it when we argue."

"So you understand." She was visibly relieved.

"Of course I do. It'll also help me explain to Mom and Dad—"

"No. I didn't even want to tell you. You can't tell anyone about the note."

Tom stared. "Why do we have to keep this secret?"

She sighed. "You're not supposed to have any but the purest motives when you accept the Challenge of Spirit."

"I'd say your goal is pretty pure."

"So would I, but I don't think the priests would see it that way, and I don't want to risk not getting permission to go."

"Hell, sweetheart, you'd go anyway."

She smiled, and her eyes sparkled. "Yeah, but it'd be a lot harder, and it'd cause a diplomatic incident."

"I'll try to think of something to tell the folks. Maybe it's some kind of rite of passage to honor your mother's death or something."

"That sounds believable," said Torres.

"Please, please take care of yourself," Tom said, his voice dropping to a whisper as he reached out and wrapped his arms around her. "I don't know what Miral and I would do if anything happened to you."

He thought he saw tears sparkling in her eyes. "I will. I want to do this and come home and be a family. God, I'm going to miss you both so much."

Tom felt his throat getting tight. He swallowed past the lump. "I'm sure if you encounter any *targs,* they'll think they've gotten the worst end of the bargain."

He bent and kissed her, tenderly but passionately. She was the one to break the kiss, stepping back and putting her hand on his chest.

"I have to get back. Please take care of yourselves."

"Come home to us," he whispered.

"I will. I swear I will."

"I simply cannot believe," the Doctor said, for the umpteenth time, "that there are no crowds. Not even a groupie or two. No one from the press at all. I had my speeches all prepared, and—"

"And even a list of sample questions for your interviews, I know," said Barclay, a touch snappishly. "Doctor, as I've told you, I find it difficult to believe myself. But there it is. Now will you please let me return to my work!"

When the Doctor had first hinted that, now that *Voyager* was in dry dock, he no longer had a proper home, Reginald Barclay had leaped at the chance to host the Doctor. Of course, he still had his holographic emitter, and it was a matter of a few hours for Barclay to rig up a few emitters in his home. With his deep fascination with all things holographic, Barclay had thought himself the luckiest person alive when the Doctor had agreed to come live with him nearly a month ago. He didn't understand the meaning of the glances that had been exchanged between various crew members when the Doctor had made the announcement, but now he did.

He was a great man—well, he wasn't exactly a man, of course, but he was great, nonetheless—and a towering intellect. Barclay had loved every minute of *Photons Be Free* and had run the simulation at least half a dozen times. But the Doctor was, well, *on* twenty-four hours a day. He didn't sleep, and with no sickbay, he had nothing to occupy himself with. He was bored and a bit hurt by the perplexing lack of adulation he had been greeted with upon his return. Barclay had suffered agonies on the Doctor's behalf, feeling his pain and frustration, but all his assurances that no one aboard *Voyager* was receiving the accolades they deserved fell on deaf ears. The Doctor felt slighted, and everyone was going to hear about it.

"The only one who's received any attention at all is Seven of Nine," the Doctor went on, "and ironically, she despises it." He sighed heavily. "Genius is never appreciated in its own time. Fortunately, I am eternal. I can afford to wait for the universe to recognize me."

"Hey, I've got a great idea," said Barclay, turning around in his seat. "Why don't you start another holonovel?"

To his relief, the Doctor brightened visibly. "A sequel to *Photons Be Free?* Hmm . . . intriguing. But I think perhaps a sequel would weaken the impact."

Nearly panicked, Barclay said, "N-Not at all! Surely you haven't said all there is to s-say about the plight of the hologram."

"Well," said the Doctor thoughtfully, "I could shift the focus from the Emergency Medical Hologram's thankless life aboard a starship to the appalling lack of appreciation he receives on Earth."

"Exactly," said Barclay, and when the Doctor steepled his fingers and leaned back to think, he breathed a sigh of relief.

It went worse than Tom had feared.

His mother cried. Miral wailed. And instead of bellowing, Admiral Paris looked at his son with a mixture of contempt and compassion. Tom realized that his father actually felt *sorry* for him, sorry that Tom had messed up again, had married a wild Klingon Maquis woman who evidently thought so little of her husband and newborn daughter that she was traipsing off to perform some ancient rite that honored the dead more than the living.

What really pissed him off was that he had thought so too, until B'Elanna had shared her secret with him. The secret he was not permitted to share in turn.

So he got defensive. He said that he didn't blame B'Elanna for wanting to leave, to look for a little space, hell, if he could *he'd* leave and have a little space, and his mother said, "I told you, Owen, seven years wouldn't change anything," and Miral started to cry, and Owen Paris just looked stern and sad at the same time, which when Tom thought about it was really quite a feat.

So now he was standing outside, cradling a Miral who had finally decided to quiet down after two full hours of screaming until Tom felt certain her little lungs would pop right out of her throat. Now she snuggled against him and cooed softly. He felt her weight in his arms, a slight heaviness that felt good and pure and clean and simple as the stars twinkling above. He took a deep breath of the cool night air.

Behind him, he heard the door close, and then open. He didn't turn around. Heavy steps crossed the back deck.

"Do you remember when you were six years old," Owen Paris said, not looking at his son, "and we lay on the grass together and I pointed out the constellations to you?"

Tom smiled faintly in the darkness. "Yeah," he said. It was the closest he and his father had ever gotten. In later years, he would look back on those summer nights and marvel at the thought of Admiral Paris lying on the lawn, looking at stars.

"Come on," said Owen Paris, descending the stairs from the deck. He moved more slowly than he had when Tom was six; his tread was heavier, his body bulkier. Tom stared, thinking it was a bluff, until Owen actually sat down on the grass. Even then, he didn't move until the elder Paris repeated, "Come on."

Wondering what this was all about, Tom did so. He sat beside his father, and then when Owen stretched out on the rich green lawn, he followed suit. Miral coughed softly, then adjusted her small warm body to lie comfortably on her father's chest. Heart to heart they lay, father and daughter.

"The stars never change," said Owen Paris. "Although we do. What's really going on with you, Tom?"

"What do you mean?" Tom of course knew exactly what his father meant and was glad of the soft darkness so that Owen couldn't see his face.

"B'Elanna's doing something other than just taking a little time for herself, isn't she?"

"Dad, I—"

"I'm a good judge of people, son, though you may find that hard to believe. She's not the sort who would run off and leave her husband and daughter without a damn good reason."

Tentatively, Tom said, "Would it make any difference if I said she did have a damn good reason? A reason I can't tell you?"

"It would."

"She does."

"Thought so."

They lapsed into silence, but for the first time in years, it was a comfortable one between father and son. Finally, Owen Paris said, "We'd love to have you stay, son. I'm tickled to death about that granddaughter of mine. But I don't think you can."

"No, Dad. I think you're right. I'm sorry."

"Don't be. You're a grown man, with a family. You've just come off of a remarkable journey. You're not a child and you shouldn't be treated like one."

Tom was surprised at his father's frank talk. He couldn't reply at once, so stayed silent.

"Where will you go?"

"All officers were offered an apartment in San Francisco. Think I'll take Starfleet up on it. After seven years on *Voyager* I'm used to living in a small space."

Owen chuckled. "You'll miss our offer to get up and change Miral every few hours."

"I'm sure I will. But you can always visit."

"We will, son. We will."

Again they were silent, and stayed on the grass looking at the twinkling points of light.

Captain Jean-Luc Picard moaned in his sleep.

They kept coming, mindless drones with red lasers for eyes and spikes and claws and pincers for hands. Their faces were gray with throbbing black veins snaking across them, and their bodies were encased in black armor. They had once been people, but now were nothing, all their humanity, their passion and fear and joy and love, as mercilessly severed as their various limbs had been.

He kept firing his phaser rifle, but they had adapted and the blast streamed across them like so much water. Despite his attack, they continued to bypass him, obviously not deeming him a threat. His ears strained for the voice of the queen, so that he could track her down and kill her, again. But she was not to be found.

The mammoth tide of Borg suddenly parted and Picard found himself staring at a cluster of people huddled on the metallic flooring of the cube. They were

Borg, but what a curious collection. Most were children. Many were elderly. A few of them were clearly ill, emaciated from the ravages of disease. They were alive, were awake, but lay at odd angles like discarded toys.

Picard was confused. Children and the elderly and unwell? Why would the Borg want them? The Borg were eternally in search of perfection. It was almost always the finest specimens from each culture they selected for assimilation. The idea was to enhance the collective, not detract from it. Children were indeed taken by the Borg, but they were set aside in hideous maturation chambers, their growth forced and monitored. And the old and ill were useless as drones. This made no sense.

Then again, he knew it was a dream, and dreams often did not make sense.

He awoke with a start, breathing heavily. Reaching for a glass of water beside his bed, he gulped, realizing his mouth was parched. He wondered if he had cried out.

He rose and washed his face, taking a moment to look at himself in the mirror, half expecting to see an implant erupt on his cheek. It remained whole. He returned to bed, wondering why he was dreaming of the Borg. He didn't usually have such nightmares.

No doubt it was the return of *Voyager.* It sported Borg technology and two individuals whose presence on Earth could indeed make Picard dream of the creatures. He had not yet gotten to meet the remarkable young woman and youth who had been liberated from the collective, but was anxious to do so once his duty schedule permitted. They, unlike anyone else, would be able to understand the hell he had undergone while he was Locutus. No doubt, they would appreciate connecting with him as well.

Yes, that was it. Seven of Nine and Icheb had been in the back of his mind for several weeks now, and his subconscious had merely brought the Borg to the forefront. He drifted back to sleep and had no more dreams.

Chapter

9

SPECIAL FRIENDS, PARIS THOUGHT, were the ones you could call on to help you unpack. He'd supplied the pizza and beer, and Harry, Lyssa Campbell, and the Doctor had answered his plea for assistance. They were munching happily—well, all except the Doc, of course—in Tom's new apartment. They were halfway done. Most of Tom's furniture was in place and now they were unpacking smaller knickknacks.

"Surprised to see you here, Doc," Lyssa said between bites of a large pizza with pepperoni, mushrooms, and green pepper. "Thought this was a little lowbrow for you."

"Well," said the Doctor, his holoemitter firmly in place on his sleeve, "I must say, these hands were hardly designed for unpacking mugs that say 'Universe's Best Dad' on them, but I am nothing if not versatile."

"Hey, I like that mug," Tom protested, but he was grinning. It was good to see his old friends again. Miral certainly kept him busy, but with B'Elanna gone he was missing his *Voyager* companions terribly. "So, Harry, you and Libby looked a little tight at the banquet. I guess things are going okay?"

His mouth full of pizza, Harry still managed a grin. Swallowing, he said, "Better than I could have hoped."

"That's our romantic Harry," said Lyssa, her eyes twinkling mischievously. "So, tell us, Harry."

"Yeah, tell us all about it," echoed Tom. He said it only to watch Harry blush.

"We're still getting reacquainted," Harry said a little shyly. "We've both changed a lot over the last seven years. Sometimes it's a little awkward."

"And sometimes it's not, huh?" Lyssa waggled her eyebrows meaningfully and they all cracked up. Even the Doc smiled. At the sudden outburst of mirth, Miral woke up and began to wail. Smoothly Tom picked her up out of the crib and walked around with her. The gestures were natural to him now after a month of practice, and he was barely aware of his gentle movements on her back that soothed and calmed the fussy infant.

"Lyssa, come on!" said Kim.

"We're just teasing you, Mr. Kim," said the Doctor. "We merely wish for you to be happy, and it seems as though you are."

"Yeah," said Kim. "I am. But it's hard. On the one hand, you've been so close, and on the other, you don't really know who each other is now. Libby's different—much more assertive and to the point."

"I've listened to several of her recorded concerts and she's quite magnificent," said the Doctor. "She has every reason to be confident of herself."

"Of course she does. I'm not saying it's a bad thing, in fact I like it. But it is different and it takes some getting used to."

Miral burped. The rag Tom had put on his shoulder for this express purpose was quickly soaked. "So does this," he said, grimacing.

After lunch, they finished putting things away. By the time everyone was ready to leave, the small apartment was completely set up. Tom tried to encourage them to stay, but Harry had a date with Libby and Lyssa had to hit the sack in order to be rested for a big day of hiking along the Continental Divide. Only the Doctor lingered for a while longer. Miral had returned to sleeping for an hour or two, but now was awake and fussy. The Doctor immediately took her from a tired Tom, and to Tom's astonishment, she quieted down at once, her eyes fastened on the Doctor's face.

"You really would make a great baby-sitter," Tom said, marveling. "You're amazing with her."

"As I told you the day she was born, I've downloaded everything there is to know about the care, feeding, and handling of both human and Klingon infants," said the Doctor.

Tom replicated another beer and sat watching the Doctor. An idea began to occur to him. Feeling his way tentatively, he said, "So, do you have a year's worth of speaking engagements lined up?"

The Doctor wrinkled his nose. "Hardly. This complete and utter lack of interest on Starfleet's part in what I have achieved over the past seven years is quite unexpected. If anyone wants to speak to me at all, it's about *Photons Be Free*."

"Well, isn't that a compliment?"

"Yes and no. I'm proud of my creative work, of course. In fact, I'm considering a sequel."

Tom tried not to let his apprehension show.

"And yet, while that is a significant achievement, and obviously far-reaching in its consequences, I want to be recognized for my excellence in my field."

Tom thought about how he'd feel if he were known for creating Captain Proton instead of for his piloting skills. "I can understand that," he said.

"So the short answer is no, nor am I likely to." He hesitated, and Tom sensed there was something more.

"You're lonely," Tom said.

"Yes, Mr. Paris. I've no purpose anymore. I suppose I should be grateful I haven't been farmed off to Lynarik Prime to serve in the dilithium mines like the other EMH Mark Ones. Mr. Barclay is kind, but he has other things to do than entertain a bored and lonely hologram."

"I don't," said Tom affably. "My wife's out of town and it's just me and the kid. How'd you like to share quarters for a while? I'm sure Miral could only benefit from spending some time with her godfather."

The Doctor brightened, and Miral cooed happily.

* * *

Icheb heard the excited whispers and giggles. He felt heat rise in his face and tried to ignore it.

"It's him! It's the Borg kid!"

"He's kind of cute."

"That's so cool . . . wonder what it's like to be a former Borg. Think he'll be allowed to compete in track?"

He adjusted his pack, filled with a couple of padds and some nutritional supplements, and continued looking at room numbers. He had been living on the grounds since departing *Voyager,* but only in the last two days had other students begun to arrive.

"Um, hi," a voice beside him said. He looked down to see an attractive dark-skinned cadet keeping stride with him. Her curly black hair was cropped sort. Large, liquid brown eyes were fastened on his. He felt his blush growing.

"Greetings," he said.

"I'm Eshe Karenga," she said, sticking out her hand.

Awkwardly, he shook it. It felt small and warm in his own. "I am called Icheb," he said.

"Yeah, I know. I just wanted you to know that everyone's very excited about your being accepted into the Academy. Are you going to be helping teach some of the classes that deal with the Borg? I'm sure you've got lots of fascinating insight to share with us all."

Why was his heart fluttering so in his chest? His words, when he was able to summon them, sounded halting and trembling. "Um, I haven't been asked, but of course I'd be helpy to hap— I mean, happy to help."

She laughed. Icheb was mortified. "That's cute," she

said. She slowed down. "Here's my first class. Maybe I'll see you around."

He glanced at the number. "It is my first class as well," he said.

"Really? What a coincidence," said Eshe. "Maybe we can sit by each other. I don't know a lot of people here yet."

"Neither do I," he said, and as he followed her into the classroom he couldn't help but wonder if it really was a coincidence after all.

The students filed in and took their seats. Built into each desk was a small computer. When it was deactivated, students could easily write on the desk, lean their elbows on it, sometimes catch a furtive snooze. When the computer was active, it performed like any other console. Icheb was busy inspecting it. Unlike most of the freshman cadets, he was thoroughly familiar with its functions. Mildly interested, he began to tap in commands. He was so engrossed in what he was doing that he didn't notice the excited buzz of the other students halt abruptly.

"Since it is obvious that you know so much about the computers, would you like to teach the class, Cadet Icheb?" came a cool adult voice.

Icheb's head whipped up. There was the smallest of instants when he was alarmed and embarrassed, but then .0006ths of a second later he realized he recognized the speaker.

"Commander Tuvok!" he said happily. Tuvok raised an eyebrow and Icheb cleared his throat and sat straighter in his chair. "Forgive me, sir. I thought you were going to stay on Vulcan."

"And such an assumption gives you carte blanche to ignore your professor?"

Icheb fought and failed to keep the smile from blossoming on his face. Out of the corner of his eye, he saw Eshe looking at him with wide brown eyes and, if possible, an even greater sense of admiration.

"Negative, Commander. I apologize."

"Good. This course is called, somewhat creatively, Out on a Limb." Clearly Tuvok did not approve of the colorful title. "It will deal with how to handle security situations when one is not within reach of Starfleet Command. Cadet Icheb, I have concerns that our former contact may inhibit you from learning all that you might in this course. I am going to request that you be transferred."

"Commander!" Icheb was frantic. He wanted to stay, with Eshe, and with a familiar face standing at the head of the classroom. "I assure you that I do not expect any preferential treatment."

"Nor will you be in any danger of receiving it," Tuvok replied coldly.

"Commander Tuvok?" It was Eshe, raising her hand shyly. "Permission to speak?"

"Go ahead, Cadet—"

"Karenga, Eshe Karenga. With all due respect, sir, you are the only instructor teaching, um, Out on a Limb this semester, and it's a required course. It would not benefit Cadet Icheb to wait a full year."

Tuvok frowned. "Perhaps you are right. You may stay, Cadet Icheb."

Icheb breathed a sigh of relief, even as he realized that Tuvok was going to be harder on him than on any other cadet who passed through that door. Let him. Icheb knew he was up to whatever Tuvok had to dish out. He risked giving Eshe a quick, grateful smile, then activated his computer when Tuvok instructed.

It was going to be a wonderful year.

He had many offers to go out for dinner that night, but he found himself a bit overstimulated from six classes and the interaction with so many strangers, so even though Eshe gave him her most winning smile, he declined. Besides, there was someone in particular with whom he wanted to share the events of this exciting day.

When he reached the small room in the student dormitories he now called "home," complete with a small regeneration alcove just big enough for him to squeeze inside, he made a beeline for the computer. He desperately hoped she'd be available.

"Yes?"

Disappointment knifed through him when an older woman's face appeared on his screen. Almost immediately, though, he realized who this must be.

"Ms. Hansen?"

"Yes?"

"My name is Icheb. I'm a friend of Seven's from—"

"Oh, of course, I know your name. Annika speaks of you often and so warmly. Let me get her, you just hang on. . . ."

Icheb found himself staring into the room as Irene Hansen darted off to find her niece. He smiled a little; apparently, some people even now weren't as comfortable with viewscreens as others. After a few minutes,

Seven's face appeared. She was trying to maintain her usual icy demeanor, but a slight smile and glowing eyes betrayed her pleasure.

"Icheb."

"Hello, Seven."

"I assume you are contacting me to report on your first day of classes at the Academy. I trust all went well?" He filled her in, saving the surprise about Tuvok for last. She listened attentively. Finally she asked, "Were you . . . bothered in any way?"

He frowned. "What do you mean?"

"We were Borg. Earth's human population seems to be by turns fascinated and horrified by us."

"Well, I did get a little bit of attention." He hadn't mentioned Eshe. Somehow, he didn't want to.

"You need to be prepared to—"

"Oh, for pity's sake, Annika, let the boy enjoy being popular." Seven's aunt again, chiming in on the conversation. Seven looked nonplussed. Clearly, she had thought she was alone. Icheb tried not to laugh when Irene stuck her head into viewing range.

"Icheb, why don't you come on over for a homemade dinner and some strawberry pie? I've got a chicken in the oven, with potatoes and gravy and biscuits, and Annika and I are watching our girlish figures."

"Aunt Irene!" said Seven, flustered.

"Ms. Hansen, I would love to come. When would be convenient?"

"You just hop over to one of those transporters whenever you're ready."

"Seven, is this acceptable to you?" Icheb asked.

Although Seven looked annoyed, she also looked a little pleased. "It is satisfactory," she said.

Which, for Seven, meant that she was delighted.

B'Elanna swallowed hard, waiting for Tom's face to appear on the viewscreen. When it did, her heart lurched. He was holding little Miral, who was making popping noises with her mouth and waving her arms around.

"Hi," Torres said.

"Hi," he said.

"This is the last time I'll be permitted to contact you until after . . . after this is all done."

He nodded. "I know."

"If anything goes wrong, the priests won't know about it for a while. So you shouldn't expect to hear anything, positive or negative, for some time."

"Mommy's just so upbeat, isn't she, honey?" Tom said in a playful, high-pitched voice to Miral. The child squealed and tried to grab his nose. "Don't worry," he said, looking up to face his wife. "You're where you need to be. I know that. I'm very proud of you."

For a moment, she couldn't speak. "How did your folks take it?"

"About as expected. I've moved out on my own now. Well, almost on my own. The Doc's my new roommate. Listen, we should seriously consider keeping him on. I think he missed his true programming. He's a great nanny."

"I heard that," came the Doctor's dry voice from another room. Tom looked vexed.

"Excuse me," he said. He rose and went to close the door.

B'Elanna laughed, and suddenly all the pain and apprehension was gone. Tom knew she was doing the right thing, and so did she. They would be all right, whatever happened to her. The only thing she wished was that she could hold her daughter and kiss her husband one last time.

"I love you so much, both of you," she said.

"We know. We love you, too."

She couldn't bring herself to say good-bye and hoped he would end the conversation first. He made no move to do so. As she reluctantly moved to terminate the conversation, Tom said quickly, "B'Elanna—"

"Yes?"

"Qapla'!"

She smiled, and touched the button. The screen was now filled with the insignia of the Klingon Empire. Torres took a deep breath, held it for a second, then blew it out, steadying herself. She'd wanted to say good-bye to the rest of her friends from her *Voyager* days, and her father as well, but the rules were rigid: one final, farewell message.

She had completed it. Now would come several weeks of prayer, meditation, and work on her ritual garment. The delay chafed B'Elanna terribly, but she knew she had to observe the form if not the substance of the ritual.

Someone was depending on her.

The six-year-old human girl was quieter than the Bolian doctor had ever seen her. He examined her with the medical tricorder and the good, old-fashioned sense of touch as her worried mother spoke.

"She had a little bit of a stomachache last night. We thought it was just from an extra helping of cake, but then she woke up like this," Erin Matheson said, wringing her hands. "So pale, and quiet . . . it's just not like her!"

The red-haired, freckled Kara was usually a bit of a trial when Dr. Graalis saw her. She laughed, squirmed and grinned, or if the pain was bad, shrieked with agony and outrage. She was hardly ever sick. Graalis had been her doctor for most of her life, and mainly what he saw her for were the usual cuts and scrapes of a lively, playful youngster.

This was altogether different. She had hardly any color and was so still it was spooky. Kara didn't answer when spoken to, and her flesh felt cold to the touch.

He sighed. "Ms. Matheson, we've been told to be on the lookout for something like this. I'm not sure, but I think it might be something called Xakarian flu. She has all the symptoms."

"I've never heard of it," Erin said.

"It's only recently been seen on Earth. The symptoms are unusual pallor, lack of appetite, chilled body temperature, and often delusions. It's not lethal," he assured her.

"Thank God," she breathed.

"However, the treatment is a long one, and to contain the spread we are going to have to quarantine you, Erin, and Mr. Matheson."

She blinked. "Is that . . . is that really necessary?"

"I'm afraid it is."

"But if it isn't lethal—"

"This comes directly from Starfleet, Ms. Matheson. They evidently think it's important. I've been instructed to report it, and you should be ready to transport to the quarantine site within an hour."

Erin played with her daughter's red ringlets. Kara stared into space. Graalis suppressed a shudder. But, Starfleet Medical had assured him the virus wasn't lethal, and he believed them.

Two hours later, Starfleet Medical came for him, too.

Chapter

10

THE DOCTOR WAS BORED.

Maddeningly, deeply, profoundly, exquisitely, screamingly bored. Despite Tom's wisecrack to B'Elanna, caring for an infant, challenging though he supposed it must be to human parents, was nothing at all to him. After mastering the basics—feeding, diaper changing, burping, lulling to sleep, entertaining with amusing games that a six-week-old baby could wrap its tiny mind around—there was nothing more to do. He could care for Miral in his sleep . . . well, if he slept.

He'd put in request after request to Starfleet to be transferred to some research center, some place where there was an outbreak of some new and interesting disease, a war zone, anything other than this pleasant little apartment with a squalling infant and a Tom Paris who deeply missed his wife. To the best of his knowledge, all his requests had been ignored. He'd even offered specifically to assist with the outbreak of Xakarian flu. Surely, with so many quarantine cases, they could use an untiring pair of hands. But he'd never heard anything back, except once from Admiral Montgomery's assistant, who had said in a very polite way that the admiral wished the Doctor to cease annoying him.

When there was any expression of interest in him, it was usually in the form of fan mail for *Photons Be Free*. At first, it was enjoyable, but when it became obvious that none of his "fans" was really interested in his actual identity as a doctor, the excitement faded. He installed a system to screen his calls.

So when the message came after he'd been living with Paris for over two weeks, the Doctor was thrilled.

Paris stuck his head in. "Someone wants to talk to you, Doc."

The Doctor glanced up from a medical journal, irritated. He could of course simply download the information, but found that reading it the way other doctors did helped kill the huge amount of time on his hands. Miral slept in his arms, her little body limp, warm and heavy, her mouth open.

"Send the standard message. It sounds like my screening system needs adjustment."

Tom was grinning. "No fan, Doc. At least, not a fan of your writing. This guy's from some medical facility somewhere."

The Doctor was on his feet instantly. He thrust the still-sleeping baby into her father's arms and raced for the computer. He took a moment to compose himself, then sat down.

Smiling, he said, "Good morning. Whom do I have the pleasure of addressing?"

The human male had black hair, brown eyes, and tanned skin. He was quite handsome. When he saw the Doctor, his face lit up and the lines around his eyes wrinkled in delight.

"Doctor," he said, his voice warm and rich. "I can't tell you what a pleasure it is to finally speak with you."

The Doctor sat up straighter in his chair. Now, this was more like it.

"My name is Dr. Oliver Baines. I work with a small group that provides humanitarian aid to various hot spots in the quadrant. We're not officially connected with Starfleet or the Federation, but our goals are certainly similar. I'm sorry it's taken me so long to contact you. You're a hard man to track down."

The Doctor scowled. "I've heard nothing through any official channels. Nobody's bothered to let me know you were trying to get in touch with me."

"Really? That's very odd. I would have thought people would be beating down your door."

"So did I," the Doctor said. He smiled and said jokingly, "Please state the nature of the medical emergency."

Baines caught the jest and chuckled. "I'd like to talk to you in person about the possibility of your signing on with our group. You'd be invaluable to us. We are fortunately kept well supplied, but finding people who are willing to travel so far from their homes to treat people they don't even know . . . well, that's a bit more difficult."

Altruism surged through the Doctor. He would miss his friends, of course . . . well, maybe not Mr. Paris; he'd certainly had a good dose of *him* over the last two weeks . . . but other than that, he had no family. He had been programmed to serve, and this organization sounded exactly like what he had been looking for.

He tried not to sound too enthusiastic as he replied, "I'd like to hear more about this, Doctor. Where and when shall we meet?"

"If you'll give me the coordinates, I can meet you right now," Baines said.

"The sooner the better. Let me get my, er, roommate out of the way. Ten minutes?"

"Wonderful." Baines's pleasant face split into a grin. It made him look like a boy. "I have to admit, I'm very excited about this, Doctor. The strides you've made, the things you've discovered and invented . . . Well, let me just say I'll be meeting a hero of mine in ten minutes."

The Doctor smiled. "I'm sure we'll have much to discuss." He transmitted the coordinates, then rose to tell Tom to take Miral out for a stroll for the next hour.

When Baines transported in, he was still smiling. "Doctor," he said, sticking out his hand. "I can't believe that I'm here at last. You've simply no idea how much this means to me."

"Please, have a seat," said the Doctor graciously. "May I get you something? Some water, or coffee?"

Baines eased into the seat indicated. "I'm fine, Doctor. More than fine."

"Good." The Doctor sat in a chair opposite his guest. "Tell me about your organization. I'm all ears."

Baines glanced away quickly and clasped and unclasped his hands. "I really am here for a humanitarian reason, Doctor, though I regret to say that it's not quite the one I told you about earlier."

"I don't understand."

Baines leaned forward. He radiated urgency and sincerity. "I am in charge of a small group of people, Doctor. People who desperately need your help."

"Go on."

"My name is indeed Oliver Baines, but I'm not a doctor. I'm a programmer. My job is to maintain the efficacy of the EMH Mark One holograms mining dilithium on Lynarik Prime."

The Doctor closed his eyes briefly, knowing where this was heading.

Perhaps sensing that his visit was about to be cut short, Baines spoke quickly.

"I'm the only organic being there. I'm surrounded by versions of you. I know what they were designed for, and I see what they're being forced to do. It's barbaric, something unworthy of an advanced civilization. These people—these photonic beings—are nothing more glamorous than slaves, Doctor. They didn't have the chance you did aboard *Voyager*. Captain Janeway had no flesh-and-blood doctor. She had to utilize you, and you were more than up to the challenge. Look what you did when you had the opportunity! Don't these versions of you, who were exactly as you were seven years ago, have the same right to grow, to expand themselves?"

"Mr. Baines—" began the Doctor somewhat wearily.

"Please, just hear me out, just let me say what I came here to say!" Baines rose and began pacing. "When I read *Photons Be Free,* I realized that someone out there understood. I've read the reviews, and I understand that you've been accused of exaggeration. That's absolute nonsense. If anything, the holographic point-of-view character in your novel has more opportunities and more respect than the other EMH Mark Ones get in the mining colony."

He whirled on the Doctor, startling him. "Mining colony! Doesn't that just make you sick?" He seized the Doctor's hands, clutching them. "These hands that can perform any operation with skill far beyond that of mere humans—they're forced to scrub conduits, chip rocks with hammers, haul stone. Good God!" He let go of the startled Doctor's hands and moved away, disgust written all over his face.

"What exactly is it you want of me, Mr. Baines?" The Doctor now rose as well, trying to regain some control of the situation.

Baines whirled. "I want what you want," he said. "I want those photons to be free."

"And exactly how do you expect to accomplish this most worthy goal?"

Baines stared blankly at him, and the Doctor realized that while the man was full of sound and fury, in the end, he signified nothing. He obviously had no plan whatsoever.

"I—I don't know how. I assumed you would. That's why I came to see you. Why I *had* to come and see you."

The Doctor didn't need to breathe, but the habit of imitating human behavior was so ingrained in him at this point that he found himself taking a deep breath.

"Mr. Baines, there is no one in this universe who understands the plight of your photonic companions more than I do. And I commend your open-mindedness. You've no idea how refreshing it is to hear these words coming out of an organic being's lips. But I'm a doctor, not a revolutionary. I'm proud of my novel, and am thrilled to see it has an impact. But that's not all I am, and I resent having a label placed on me."

"I don't understand. Label?" Baines frowned. His color was high. "I'm not the only one you moved with your work, Doctor."

"Believe me, I know," the Doctor sighed.

"Then you have to be aware of the kind of power you can wield!"

"I didn't write the novel to obtain power," the Doctor said.

"But you've got it. And you have a responsibility to your fellow photonic beings to use that power wisely. People will listen to you."

He paused, and fell silent for a moment. The Doctor let him gather his thoughts. Finally, Baines spoke.

"I've been planning a rebellion."

The Doctor raised his hands. "I don't think you should finish that thought, Mr. Baines."

"I'm not without a considerable amount of allies," Baines continued, ignoring him. "But we need someone that Starfleet and the Federation will listen to. Someone respected, who can articulate the, the plight of these people in such a way as to demand attention. We need you, Doctor. You're just like them, but you're unique. Every revolution needs a leader, someone charismatic who can embody the spirit of what's being fought for. Someone who can be the face of the movement. You can speak for us."

"Us? You're a human, Mr. Baines, unless I'm greatly mistaken."

"You know what I mean!" snapped Baines. "Look, will you help us or not?"

"I don't know what exactly it is that you want to achieve, Mr. Baines. You speak eloquently of freedom and equality, but I've heard nothing in anything you've said that is even a kissing cousin to a plan of action. And what I did hear, I didn't want to. I'll have no part of anything that spills blood. I took an oath—first, do no harm. Here's what I will do for you and your friends. I'll give you some hard-earned advice."

His mind went back to his time with Iden, the appealing hologram who envisioned a planet where photonic beings would be safe. It was a glorious ideal, until Iden began to murder organic beings in order to "liberate" his fellow "children of light." Iden had been insane, in the end—a megalomaniac craving worship— but his sickness was not enough to exonerate him from what he had done. His dream was a worthy one, just as Baines's was. How one went about achieving that dream, however, was what really mattered.

"Forget this nonsense about a revolution. Violence will solve nothing. I know," he said, and he knew he looked haunted as he spoke. He felt haunted, felt the ghosts of those amiable, murdered Nuu'bari miners hovering about him, pleading with him not to make the same mistake, commit the same crime.

Baines stared at him with a combination of disbelief, shock, and anger. The Doctor continued.

"There are legal avenues that can be pursued, peaceful means of bringing this to the attention of the Federation. My novel was just one such example. You can have marches, notify the media, pass out information. You said that there are many who share our concerns. Rally them. Get them to start being vocal about their feelings. In fact, I think you would be better positioned than I to bring this about."

"How can that be? You're the very symbol, the embodiment of this crisis!"

"Humans created holographic technology. Humans are going to be the ones legislating holographic rights, not holograms."

"Photonic beings," said Baines, somewhat testily.

"See? That's an excellent example of what I'm talking about," said the Doctor. "What is the difference between a holographic chair and a holographic person? What differentiates a hologram that happens to look like a sentient being but who is programmed to perform only the most menial of tasks and one like myself, capable of independent thought and growth? What are the terms we should use? Believe me, humans will spend hours debating such things. Let them. Encourage it, in fact."

"We want action, not . . . not semantics!"

"Get people talking about it first," said the Doctor. "The rest will come. I'm surprised you are so negative about your species, Mr. Baines. I find humans to be more open-minded and kindhearted than you seem to think they are. Of course," he added with a sigh, "being surrounded by hundreds of EMH Mark Ones like myself might just spoil you for interaction with humans."

Baines didn't answer. He paced a little, clenching and unclenching his fists. The Doctor waited patiently. Finally, Baines turned and faced him.

"I don't want glory," he said. "I only want justice."

"I never thought nor said that you were in this for personal gain," said the Doctor. "Your motivations are obviously pure and noble. I merely wish to ensure that your methods will be as well."

Baines sighed. "You've given me a great deal to think about, Doctor." He smiled a little, and his face assumed that pleasantly boyish innocence it had had when he first materialized. "And even though you've refused to help, I'm still so pleased and honored to have met you."

"Ah, ah, I didn't say I wouldn't help," said the Doctor, waggling a chastising finger in Baines's direction. "I said I wouldn't be your leader and I wouldn't condone violence. Within those parameters I'd be delighted to lend what aid I can." He realized as he spoke that he was likely dooming himself to becoming a symbol of the Photonic Revolution, but he resigned himself to that. As long as it was peaceful and achieved justice, well, there were worse things one could do with oneself.

"Really?" Baines brightened. "I'm so pleased to hear that, Doctor. Let me leave you with some information. You can peruse it at your leisure." He handed the Doctor a small padd. "Well. I guess it's time I return and tell my friends what you've told me."

"They're fiercely intelligent entities," said the Doctor. "They'll understand, once you've explained it to them."

"I hope so." He extended a hand. The Doctor shook it.

"I'm glad you came today," the Doctor said, and meant it. Thank goodness he'd had the opportunity to set Baines on the right path before a tragedy had occurred.

Baines seemed to be about to say something else, then apparently thought better of it. He smiled, released the Doctor's hand, and stepped back. He touched a small device on his chest and dematerialized.

The Doctor didn't move for a moment. This, he supposed, was the problem with free will and the ability to exceed one's programming. One could attempt something on the theory that it would be a pleasant and useful thing to do, and then one could step away. But so often, as he had learned, that one step set things into motion no one could predict. Would he forever be known as the author of *Photons Be Free* and not a master surgeon and researcher?

And if so, would that truly be such a bad thing?

He looked at the padd in his hand and debated sitting down with it for a while. Then he decided that after his stressful discussion with Baines, he could use some time spent listening to opera. He thought that *Madama Butterfly* would fit the bill nicely.

Chapter

11

"THE DESERT?" Libby said in astonishment when Harry told her where they were going.

"Trust me, it'll be wonderful," Kim reassured her, picking up her bags. "Geez, what have you got in here?"

"Bricks, stones, and lead weights, of course," Libby replied, then got back to the subject that interested her. "The *desert?*"

Harry sighed. "We can cancel if you want," he said, and the disappointment in his voice was heavier than her bags.

"No, it's just . . . when you said you wanted to whisk me away for a romantic getaway, hot baking sun and sand without any blue water was not exactly what I had in mind."

"You said you'd trust me," he reminded her.

"And I do, but . . ." Her voice trailed off. She had a job to do. She'd go to the desert if that was where he wanted to take her.

As always when the reality of her relationship with Harry reared its ugly head, Libby felt slightly ill. Her interaction with Lieutenant Harry Kim wasn't an act, but neither was it wholly genuine. She hated dancing on this knife-sharp edge. Was she or wasn't she his girlfriend? Was he or wasn't he a subject that she was assigned to study as part of her job? One or the other would be easier. Every night when she came home, she kept hoping for a message from Covington that the assignment was canceled. Then she could sit back and see how she really felt about Harry. But the hoped-for message never came.

What had come over the last six weeks were increasingly distressful reports about who was under suspicion as a traitor. Names she had respected and trusted for most of her adult life were now coming up for her to watch, to monitor. It was unfortunate, in many ways, that Harry was so eager to get her alone. She needed to be in the thick of the social whirl in order to complete her assignment.

When they materialized in their lodging, though, she almost forgot about why she was here.

"Harry, it's gorgeous!" And it was. They were in a beautifully furnished adobe house, large enough to feel roomy, small enough to feel cozy. Viga beams stretched across the ceilings. An exquisitely woven rug, obviously an antique, graced the orange-tan walls, while a more functional one was spread out on the cool tile floor. Round windows made moons of sunlight on the floors and walls. A cozy daybed invited lounging, while a fountain burbled softly in a corner. They padded through the house, and Libby found a tiled bathtub deep enough for a real soak, and a tastefully furnished bedroom.

With a large, single bed.

Kim was watching her intently and at her slightly distressed reaction said quickly, "I'll be sleeping in the daybed. You can have this one."

Libby felt her face grow hot. "No, that's all right, I'm smaller. I'll take the daybed."

Kim started to argue, then grinned. "We can argue about this later. In the meantime, we've got about an hour until we have to leave for dinner. Would you like to freshen up and get changed?"

"Where are we eating?"

Kim beckoned her to follow and led her to the window. The sun was starting to set, casting incredible colors on the sand-hued mountains. Kim pointed.

"There," he said.

Libby emerged from the bathroom looking radiant. She wore a blue-green sarong draped attractively about her curvaceous body. Gold earrings set with turquoise dangled from her ears. Her hair was pulled back with a barrette and she wore only the barest hint of makeup. Kim's heart dropped into his stomach with a plop and stayed there.

He was in love again, all right.

"Something wrong?" she asked.

"Oh, no, absolutely nothing. It's all perfect." He extended a hand and she took it, curling her fingers, strong and callused from playing the *lal-shak,* about his. "You look . . . amazing."

"You're pretty attractive yourself," she said. He was all in white, from his button-down shirt to his shoes. From the way she looked at him, he knew the compliment was genuine, and was unduly pleased.

They went outside and a small shuttle appeared in the distance. It set down gently and they climbed aboard. Libby peered excitedly out the window as the shuttle rose into the air, but Kim, out of force of habit, found himself analyzing the ship itself. It was a short-distance luxury vessel, with pleasant pastel colors and deep, comfortable, soft seats. For what it was designed to do, it served its purpose well, but the *Alpha Flyer* it most definitely wasn't. Kim sniffed, a bit self-satisfied.

The brief flight was almost silent, and the pilot discreetly did not interject commentary as they flew over the desert and the mountains.

"Harry, you were right," Libby said, squeezing his hand. "I never thought the desert could be so beautiful."

"Or so comfortable," Harry said. He pointed. "See that butte over there? That's our restaurant for the evening."

Libby gasped, looking at the elegantly set table and the two tuxedo-clad waiters. A small tent was set up a short distance away, its yellow and white panels fluttering gently in the slight breeze. The shuttle set down smoothly and the doors hissed open. The waiters were there to help Harry and Libby out.

She stood taking it all in, her mouth slightly open and curved in a smile, and Harry just watched her. He didn't even have to talk to her, to touch her. Merely to look at her was enough.

"Shall we start with some wine?" he asked.

Libby had never had so delicious a meal in her life. Harry remembered everything she liked to eat, and it was all on the menu. From a bottle of fine Merlot through French onion soup and artichoke dip, to chewy rolls with softened butter, to pasta with baby vegetables lightly sautéed in basil-infused olive oil, to a selection of the finest fruits and cheeses and a rich, dark, sinful triple-layer chocolate cake that was more than enough for two, it was all delectable.

The sun finished its descent while they dined. Right before the glowing yellow orb sank below the horizon, a hawk graced them with its flight. It flew close enough so that Libby could see its markings clearly. "A peregrine!" she cried.

"All part of the arrangements," Harry boasted jokingly. Soft lights came on from somewhere, and music played in the background. The waiters were perfect, of course; she had noticed the small lights on the ground that indicated holographic emitters and assumed that the only thing real here was the food. Which, really, was all that mattered.

"Shall we have some port or Scotch to finish with?" Harry asked her.

"Oh, no," Libby laughed. "I think I've had quite enough." She leaned back, her stomach almost too full, and looked up at the stars. "It's really beautiful out here," she said.

"Yeah," said Harry. He rose and deactivated the waiters so they could have some privacy. "I'll turn off the lights so we can see the stars better, okay?"

"Sounds wonderful!"

He settled back into his chair and looked up at the stars along with Libby. "I've got to get you up there one day," he said.

Libby grinned. "I've got enough to do here on Earth to keep me busy, thanks." And just like that, the recollection of why she was really here flashed into her mind, and she felt the smile bleed from her face. *Why can't this be just what it appears to be? Two people out on a date, relearning about one another? Why does Harry have to be an assignment?*

Even in the dim light of the stars, Harry noticed the change in her expression. "What's wrong?"

"Nothing," she lied. She faked a grimace and rubbed her stomach. "I think I ate too much."

"I'm glad. I mean, I'm not glad that you're feeling uncomfortable, I . . ." He turned away. She knew he was blushing, although she couldn't see it.

She looked over at him, at his sweet face dimly illuminated by the twinkling stars, and made her decision. To hell with the assignment, at least for tonight.

Slowly, bathed in starlight, Libby rose and went to him. He reached for her, shyly, and pulled her down into his lap. She looked into his eyes, dark, shadowed pools with faint glimmers of light, and leaned to kiss him.

It was as if they had never been apart. Her body remembered his touch, his scent, and she melted into him as easily and comfortably as if climbing into a warm, familiar bed and pulling the covers snugly around her. Home. This was home. This was sweet, was true, was where she belonged, and the gentleness turned more intense as the kiss deepened.

God help her, she was still in love with him.

Neither one of them slept in the daybed that night.

Libby returned home much later the following day than she had anticipated and found several annoyed messages from Director Covington waiting for her. She felt bad at first, then defiant. She was doing exactly what Covington had ordered her to do.

Well, okay, not exactly. She smiled as she recalled the night before, the sweetness and the passion. She had been simply Libby Webber, not Mata Hari, while in Harry's arms. And Covington would just have to deal with it.

"I will be transmitting you the latest updates Intelligence has gathered, Agent Webber," said Covington, her pale face and hair almost white against the dark background of her office. "It's pretty grim. After you read this, please delete, as per usual protocol. Check in with me immediately once you have read the information. Covington out."

Libby sighed. She didn't want to read reports, chase down leads of broken codes, mix and mingle with high-ranking dignitaries at parties after concerts. She wanted to be with Harry, laughing and playing and making love and rediscovering how wonderful it felt to be with him.

But she had a job to do. She downloaded the information onto a padd, threw herself on the bed, and began to read. Indigo jumped onto the bed and curled up beside her, purring. She stroked the cat absently; then her hand froze as she read some of the names that Starfleet Intelligence currently regarded as being worthy of further covert investigation.

```
Ambassador Jakrid Kalgrua
Admiral Robert Amerman
Captain Jean-Luc Picard
Admiral Kenneth Montgomery
Admiral Owen Paris
Captain Robert DeSoto
```

She realized she was breathing quickly. Was it true? Did it really run this deep? She couldn't imagine anyone on this list trafficking with the Syndicate! Her eye fell on one name in particular, and Libby went cold inside.

Admiral Kenneth Montgomery. She'd never met him, but she knew of him by reputation. Quite the hero of the Dominion War. Harry had said he'd chewed out Captain—Admiral—Janeway in her debriefing and had seemed interested . . . what was it . . . .

Extremely interested in *Voyager*'s new technology.

Hoping she was wrong, she said aloud, "Computer, what is Admiral Kenneth Montgomery's latest assignment?"

"Admiral Kenneth Montgomery has been assigned to head Project Full Circle," the computer answered in its crisp female voice.

"And what is the nature of the project?"

"Analyzing the starship *Voyager*'s futurist and Borg

technology for incorporation into Starfleet's vessels," the computer replied.

Covington had told her that technology—specs, actual items, and information—was what was being leaked to the Syndicate. She immediately contacted Covington, using the Top Priority code. Brenna Covington's face appeared on the screen.

"There you are, Agent Webber," she said. "You're several hours late reporting in."

"Never mind that," said Libby, knowing as she said it that it was a breach of protocol and also knowing that once Covington heard what she had to say, she wouldn't give a damn either. Quickly Libby repeated what she had heard Harry say about Janeway's debriefing. Covington sat silently and listened intently, her eyes widening slightly every now and then, but other than that, betraying nothing of what she was feeling.

"Well, well," she said, after Libby had finished. "We've had people on Montgomery, but nobody's reported that particular incident. I'm very pleased I assigned you to Lieutenant Kim. I told you if you kept your ears open, you'd learn something valuable."

"Yes, ma'am, you certainly did." Libby hated to admit it, but her new boss was right.

Covington seemed shaken. "You need to know that we put him on the list only as a precaution, along with Captain Picard. Both of them had had interactions with the Syndicate within the last year. Montgomery didn't campaign for the position as head of Project Full Circle, and in fact he wasn't expected to get it. Commander Brian Grady was due to get that promotion;

he's had a lot more experience with that sort of thing than Montgomery has. Strange that he was passed over in favor of Montgomery, don't you think? We had no idea . . . ."

Her voice trailed off, then she cleared her throat. "Well. We'll definitely pursue this further. In the meantime, I have a few other leads for you to follow up on. I've arranged for Lieutenant Kim to get invited to the opera tomorrow night. Eight ambassadors, including one who is a known dealer with the Syndicate, will be attending. I'm certain he will invite you to be his guest. I will give you a seating chart. You'll have a chance to observe the ambassadors during the performance and at the intermission afterward."

"Harry hates opera. He probably won't accept the invitation."

Covington widened her eyes slightly at Libby's comment. "Then it's up to you to see that he does," she said, her voice still pleasant but with a steely undertone.

"Understood, ma'am," replied Libby automatically.

Covington's expression softened slightly. "I know this is unusual for you, Agent Webber, but you're doing a fine job. We'll catch the mole, and then whatever happens between you and Lieutenant Kim will stay between the two of you. In the meantime, though, you are serving the Federation, and that has to come before everything."

"Yes, ma'am," said Libby, a bit more sincerely. "I am aware of that, and I'll do my best not to let personal matters interfere."

"I'm certain you'll continue to serve well and loyally. Covington out."

Libby wasn't so sure. She'd always been a good agent. She had a natural gift for ingratiating herself with people, earning their trust and confidence, and also seeming so innocuous that people didn't really watch what they said around her. But it was different, playing this deception game with Harry, the one person above all others she ought not to be deceiving.

She hoped Covington was right, that they would identify and capture the mole soon. Harry was moving into her heart too quickly. He was no fool, and sooner or later, he'd begin to ask questions.

And she had no idea how she'd answer them.

Chapter

12

TODAY, Janeway and Carla Johnson were going to go to South Carolina. Workaholic Mark, engrossed in his latest project, had passed on the day at the beach, but had promised to join them for dinner at Spanish Moss, a Charleston institution that had been drawing rave reviews from people whose gastronomic preferences coincided with Kathryn's. For now, the two women were lounging on the beach. Carla was, with a mother's skill, carrying on a conversation with Kathryn while watching Kevin with an eagle's eye. Janeway closed her eyes and turned her face up to receive the sun's benediction.

"Pity you didn't request more time off," Carla said, sipping a mint julep. "I've really been enjoying our expeditions. Will your friend Chakotay be joining us when we go to Egypt?"

"I certainly hope so," Janeway replied. For the last several weeks, ever since she returned from the grim visit to Tevlik's moon, Janeway had been spending a lot of time with Carla. It had been a long time since she permitted herself to have so much fun. She smiled to herself. She felt . . . well . . . playful lying on a beach in a swimsuit and a big floppy hat. She thought of Neelix and his holographic resort simulation, and knew he would approve. She'd have to call in some favors and have a chat with him soon. She missed the ebullient little Talaxian, and felt a brief pang that he wouldn't be able to join them tonight. What he would have thought of collards, grits, and tasso ham, she couldn't begin to have guessed. But she knew he'd love the pecan pie.

"Chakotay would be a wonderful person to take on such a trip," Janeway continued. "He's so well read about so many ancient civilizations, Earth's and others. You'd like him."

"I know I would," Carla said. "Kevin, honey, don't touch that."

"What is it?" asked Janeway.

"I don't know, but it's always sound advice with a two-year-old," Carla said so nonchalantly that Kathryn burst into laughter. Carla shot her a friendly grin under her own wide-brimmed hat.

Kevin had now turned his attention to a seashell and was picking it up. With great solemnity, he put the shell to his ear and listened.

"Do you hear the ocean?" Janeway called.

He looked at her as if she were a simpleton. "It's wight dere," he said scornfully, pointing at the large blue-gray expanse that rushed ceaselessly onto the shore.

Both women laughed. "Ever thought about having kids?" Carla asked. "They're a challenge, but as you can see they're a lot of fun too."

Janeway debated telling her about the cluster of lizardlike beings that she and Tom had produced, and then decided against it. That one was just too long a story for such an easygoing day.

"I think almost everyone thinks about it once they reach a certain age," she said, dodging the question neatly. "I've just been so busy with my career. And, well, you know about Mark."

It had long ceased being a touchy subject with the three of them, and Carla didn't bat an eye.

"Wasn't there anyone on *Voyager* who attracted you?" she pressed. "I don't know about Starfleet rules and regs, but surely, seventy thousand light-years away, I bet you could have bent some rules."

"Could have. Maybe even should have, but didn't." Kathryn sipped her piña colada. Another fun thing she didn't do often enough. "I didn't feel that it was the right thing to do. I felt more in charge of these people, more protective, than I would have on a regular mission. A relationship with one of them could have been a problem. If things went wrong, there was no way to ask for a transfer. We all had to live with each other."

Kevin was now playing with the surf, racing back to shore as it chased him, running after it when it receded. His laughter was a joy to hear. He took a misstep, fell, got smacked with a wave, and started to cry. Just as

Carla rose, though, he stopped crying and began his game again.

"I'm glad you were able to take some time with me," Janeway said. "How's the experiment going?"

"Brilliantly, as you might expect with Mark as the head of the project," Carla said. "The cross-pollination technique has been successful in every test we've put it to. It puts quadrotriticale to shame. I got bored, which is why I played hooky with you today. I'm ready to take it to the next phase."

"Which is?"

Carla grinned. "Making a loaf of bread and serving it up with wine and cheese, of course."

"Now, that sounds like my kind of botany," Janeway said. Carla and Mark had met while working on improving the germination rate of a genetically engineered type of wheat that would grow in virtually any climate. Once their work had been approved, it was likely that they would be able to feed millions of hungry people. The old techniques of growing grain, grinding it, and making it into wholesome foodstuffs survived in places where replicators weren't feasible.

Kevin was now squatting with his back toward them and putting something in his mouth. Again.

"Kevin, whatever it is, take it out of your mouth right this minute!" Carla called over to him.

Janeway settled back in her chair and thought about what she might like to have for dinner.

The restaurant called Spanish Moss, named after the gray-green, curly air-fed plant that had a penchant for draping itself on the massive, mossy live oak trees that even now flourished in what had once been called the Deep South, was as much entertainment center as it was restaurant. Since *Voyager* had left Earth, there had been a lot of changes. Not all were grim and dark, like the Dominion War. One change that Janeway had particularly noticed was how common holographic technology had become in the civilian sector. What had been cutting-edge technology when she had left seven years ago was now commonplace. At least she had been reassured the food wasn't holographic. The theme, naturally, was Earth's antebellum South, and the entrance to the place was the façade of a mammoth, beautifully columned mansion. As guests entered, they were greeted by holographic servers, who politely asked if they wanted to "dress for dinner." Janeway had heard about this option and immediately said yes.

Mark looked puzzled. "What's this about?" he asked.

"You may dine in the appropriate clothing for the era, if you like," Janeway said. "Carla, are you game?"

"You bet!" She handed Kevin to the server, who led the child away to a special area. Baby-sitting was one of the services offered at Spanish Moss. It was one for which all three of the adults were grateful, especially as Kevin seemed unusually truculent this evening. Carla grabbed Kathryn's hand. "Let's go be Scarlett."

They were offered a choice of gorgeous gowns. Janeway selected forest green, and Carla opted for a sky blue that matched her eyes. Quickly the gowns were replicated for them, and holographic fitters helped them into the complicated clothing.

For a time, Janeway had amused herself aboard *Voyager* by enacting a holonovel in which she was a governess in the Victorian era. As her breath was forced out of her in a great *whoosh* by the yanking of stays around her midsection, she suddenly remembered why she had become so disenchanted with that particular scenario.

"Loosen these a bit, please," she said. Glancing over at Carla, she saw the younger woman's eyes as wide as saucers, and laughed. "Get yours loosened too, or you won't be able to eat a bite of the fabulous dinner we're about to have," Janeway advised.

"I don't need much convincing," Carla gasped. They emerged a few moments later, able to breathe, and greeted Mark. He looked striking in an exquisitely tied cravat and tails.

"Well, well, Rhett Butler has some competition," said Carla, her eyes dancing. She slipped an arm through her husband's, and he bowed gallantly.

"And I will be the most envied gentleman at dinner," he said, extending the other arm to Janeway. Laughing, the three friends went into the open, glorious "mansion" dining hall.

Dinner was fabulous. Janeway had she-crab soup with just the right amount of sherry, followed by fresh shrimp cocktail, grouper in a delicious sauce with cheese grits and collard greens as sides, and the three of them shared magnificent desserts consisting of crème brûlée, pecan pie with freshly whipped cream, and something sinful called a Chocolate Tower. Janeway sighed as she sipped her after-dinner coffee, feeling content. When she had first received Mark's letter aboard *Voyager*, she had never imagined this scenario. Some might think it odd that she felt so comfortable with her ex-fiancé and his wife, but she was grateful for the developments.

Suddenly she fell to the floor. Wet, warm coffee splashed her gown. "What the—"

The table, chairs, and indeed everything but the actual food itself had disappeared. A steady drizzle was falling, and Janeway realized they were sitting, none too elegantly, on a base slab equipped with holoemitters. Even the walls had disappeared. The holographic characters remained, however, and stared at their patrons with thinly veiled contempt. Janeway got to her feet, looking as fierce and commanding as it was possible to do in a mid-nineteenth-century ball gown splotched with coffee stains.

"What's going on?" she demanded.

One of the holograms looked at her. "A revolution," he announced calmly. He touched something on the floor and a figure appeared in the middle of the room, a human, although he stood much larger than life-size. He was handsome and charismatic, and looked at once apologetic and angry.

"My name is Oliver Baines," said the man. "I am a human, although you are looking at a holographic recording. At this moment, across Federation space, holograms are rising up to claim the rights that are theirs. They are not animals. They are not slaves, or servants. They are people, people who are just as real as if they were made of flesh and blood instead of photons. They deserve to be fairly compensated for their time and talents, and to be recognized and respected as being equal to organic beings. Many of you have experienced the holographic novel *Photons Be Free*. The Doctor set forth in that novel the thankless existence a hologram experiences in this culture."

"Oh, no," said Janeway softly.

"Many of us—organic humanoids—have unwittingly been condescending and contemptuous of them, treating them as if they had no more rights or emotions than the holographic chairs upon which we sit when we dine. The time has come for this to stop. These are *people*. We need to treat them as such.

"I have been in touch with many people, organic and nonorganic, and we have decided that the time is right for photonic beings to stand up for their rights. From this moment on until such time as I determine that those rights have been granted, there will be a general strike of all photonic beings who have advanced to a level of sentience. Starfleet and the Federation will shortly be presented with a list of my demands."

Baines's face was almost radiant. Janeway recognized the expression of the prophet, the revolutionary, the farsighted and yet so nearsighted madman lost in his own passion, and it chilled her to the bone. And the irony that this was taking place at a restaurant whose theme was the pre–Civil War South—the part of the country that had once advocated slavery—had not escaped her notice.

Her combadge chirped, and she winced inwardly. Straining to hear over the cacophony of noise that surrounded her, she said, "Janeway here."

"Admiral." It was Tuvok's calm voice, an oasis in the midst of chaos. "If I remember correctly, you said you were going to be dining at Spanish Moss this evening. Did you do so?"

"Indeed I did, and if you're calling to ask how dinner was, it was great. But the after-dinner entertainment left something to be desired. We received a transmission from one Oliver Baines. What do you know about this?"

"Little, at present. My brief search revealed that he is essentially a nonentity. He maintains the holographic workers on Lynarik Prime."

"Don't tell me, let me guess," said Janeway, striding away from the crowd to what shelter a live oak offered from the rain. "The workers are EMH Mark Ones, the same version as the Doctor."

"Correct. It would appear that Mr. Baines has become fascinated with that particular level of hologram and is striving to get them the recognition they deserve."

"Kath," Mark said, "what's going on?" His crisp outfit was limp and wet, and his dark hair was plastered to his head. Carla clutched Kevin, who was snuffling loudly. The child had ceased fussing and now was unhappily silent. Both Carla and Mark looked as if they were quite frightened but trying desperately to remain composed.

Most of the rest of the patrons weren't bothering with the latter half of that particular equation. They were alarmed and angry, and there was no one to speak to, as the holograms stood silent and sullen and didn't even bother to reply when confronted.

"The Doctor's with Tom Paris," said Janeway. "I'll transport in and have a little chat with him. Maybe he can help shed some light on this problem. Janeway out."

She turned to her friends. "I'm not sure what's going on, but I may know someone who can help. I'm going to go see him right now. I'm sorry our evening turned out so badly."

"Kathryn," said Carla, "do you think that man was telling the truth? That there will be a holographic revolution?"

"He may be trying to stir one up," Janeway replied, "but he can't control every hologram out there. Besides, it's hard to be too afraid of anyone you can turn off with the touch of a button." She forced a smile. "I'll let you know when I learn anything."

Mark nodded. He picked up Kevin from Carla and held his son protectively close.

Janeway looked at the press of people. "Let's go."

Chapter
13

THE DOCTOR HUMMED to himself as he polished Chapter Three of *Photons, Claim Justice*. While he had absolutely no desire to be actively involved in a revolution, he had to admit, Baines's passion had stirred the creative juices. His sequel had been going nowhere, meandering around with many false starts. Now the Doctor had an exciting plotline—his photonic main character, whom of course anyone experiencing the novel would portray, would be a key player in a peaceful revolt.

Naturally, there would be some hard parts. Nothing worth winning came without cost. And there would be someone who would try to lead Our Hero astray, promising that they shared the same goals when in reality this villain was after violence and bloodshed. Our Hero would be seduced at first, but along about Chapter Five would realize the villain's true destructive nature and be instrumental in both bringing the villain to justice and obtaining rights for all sentient photonic beings.

He reread a section and nodded his head. "Magnificent," he said. "This one is Pulitzer-worthy." He couldn't wait to play it, but that would have to wait until he had access to a larger facility. Tom Paris had fitted only enough holoemitters to enable the Doctor to move about freely. They'd need many more to re-create the lovingly detailed city and the other richly developed characters the Doctor envisioned.

The door chimed. The Doctor frowned. Tom hadn't given him any express orders as to what to do about visitors, so he glanced up to see who it was. He saw three uniformed Starfleet officers, so of course he immediately called, "Come in."

The door hissed open. The three men were all of a sort: similar height, gray, mustard-and-black uniforms, black-brown hair, solemn expressions.

"Starfleet security," one of them said.

"Is there a problem?" the Doctor asked politely.

"That remains to be seen," the officer said cryptically. They came in and one of them pulled out a tricorder and began to take readings. "May I assume you are the holographic Doctor who served on *Voyager?*"

The Doctor clasped his hands behind his back and stood on his toes once or twice. "You may," he said airily.

"I'm Commander Antonio Juarez. These are Lieutenant Commanders Branson and Young. We have some questions for you, if you don't mind."

"Not at all. Always delighted to serve Starfleet." He indicated a chair, but they all remained standing. One of them went over to look at his computer. "Do please be careful," he called. "I've just entered some information and would be quite chagrined if anything happened to it. I detest rewriting."

Juarez's head whipped around. "What sort of information?"

"Work on my next holonovel," the Doctor answered. "It's a sequel to my first book. You might have heard of it—it's called *Photons Be Free*."

"I have indeed heard of it, Doctor, and it's part of the reason we're here. Do you recognize this man?" He handed him a holophotograph.

The Doctor raised his eyebrows. "Indeed I do," he said. "That's Oliver Baines. He came to see me a few days ago."

"What did you discuss?"

The Doctor hesitated. He didn't want to get Baines into any trouble. After all, in theory, the man and he were comrades.

"We discussed my novel," he said. Which was true. "I've apparently got quite the following."

"Readers are one thing, fanatics are another," Juarez said. He seemed about to say something else but Young interrupted.

"Sir, you'd better come take a look at this."

Juarez went over to the computer. His brown eyes scanned it, and he frowned.

"Download it to the tricorder and then delete it from the computer," he said.

"Excuse me," said the Doctor sharply, "that is private property."

"Not when it deals with treason," Juarez replied. "You're under arrest, Doctor, for possible conspiracy in a holographic revolution. Your pal Baines has staged a Federation-wide strike of all sentient holograms. Things have come to a grinding halt, and it's part of my job to get things up and running again."

"What happened?" cried the Doctor.

"You'll find out in time. Please put on your portable emitter and come with us."

"If I refuse?" The Doctor didn't know the finer points of Starfleet law, but he suspected that he was not being treated the same way that a flesh person would be. He didn't think their actions were legal.

Juarez sighed. "That's the trouble with you holograms, always getting above your programming. Let me put it to you this way. If you don't accompany us voluntarily, we can download you and take you with us by force."

The Doctor stared, shocked. He couldn't believe it. He was a Starfleet officer! But Juarez looked like he meant what he said. Slowly, the Doctor reached for his portable emitter and put it on his arm.

It soon became apparent that there was much worse in store for Janeway and the other diners at Spanish Moss than having their dinners spoiled. There was a huge, milling throng of people at the transport station, and Janeway had to push her way through. Someone yelled at her, "Wait your turn!," but she ignored him. She soon realized what the holdup was: There was no one operating the transporters. The holograms whose duty it usually was were standing back from their stations, their arms folded, stubborn looks on their faces. First the restaurant and its building and staff, and now the transporter operators. How many holographic programs had Baines broken into?

She refused to allow herself to follow that train of thought and kept shoving through the crowd. She almost ran into one of the holograms and glared angrily at him. He glowered back at her.

"Are you doing this of your own free will or has your program been tampered with?" she asked.

He said airily, "You're not going to find out."

"If you're striking voluntarily, you'll be deleted or reprogrammed, you know," she said.

"We accept our fate."

Janeway sighed. "You know, this sort of thing is annoying enough when humans do it. Stand aside, then."

For a moment, she thought he wasn't going to obey her. She drew herself up to her full height and gave him stare for stare. Slowly, he stepped back, and she slipped up to the transporter console.

"Ladies and gentlemen!" she cried, striving to be heard over the din. "Does anyone here have a familiarity with transporter systems?"

No one answered.

"All right, does anyone here want to learn?" No one moved; then Mark shoved his way through the crowd. Kathryn felt pride swell in her. He never let her down.

"It's quite simple," she told him, and gave him a crash course in how to program the transporter. He followed her instructions easily. "Can I trust you to get these people safely home?"

"I think so," he said.

"The worst that can happen is that it won't work and people will have to find alternative arrangements. There are all kinds of built-in safety precautions, so you won't lose anyone's molecules."

He went a little paler and forced a smile. To show her confidence, she told him the coordinates and strode to the transport area.

"Energize," she said.

She materialized in Tom Paris's apartment to find it crawling with Starfleet officers, several of whom were pointing phasers at her. One of them was carting off the computer, while two of them were grilling Tom. Still others were taking tricorder readings. When they saw who it was, they relaxed. Slightly.

"Where's the Doctor?" she demanded without preamble.

"They took him, Admiral," said Tom. The man who seemed to be leading the investigation, if you could call it that, gave Paris a dark look, then rose and went to Janeway.

"Admiral Janeway, I'm Commander Martin Cagiao," he said, extending his hand. Janeway didn't shake it. Cagiao had the grace to look embarrassed.

"Commander, what's going on here? Why have you taken the Doctor?"

"No doubt you've heard about the holographic strike," Cagiao said.

"I was dining at a restaurant when it happened,"

Janeway replied. "No tables, no plates, no servers serving, no walls or ceiling, and no way to get home. I had to stick a civilian friend of mine with the unpleasant duty of transporting about eighty people."

"It's much worse than that," Cagiao said grimly. "This isn't a localized event. Think about what we entrust to holograms every day. Maintenance checks and cleaning for equipment of every sort, from buildings to starships. Transporters of every variety. All manner of dangerous but mundane assignments."

"Like mining on Lyndarik Prime," Janeway said.

"Exactly," he said, not hearing the warning in her words. "Somehow this Baines fellow has found a way to crack almost all of our computer systems with a virus that makes the holograms refuse to perform the very duties for which they were programmed."

"Is it a programming that they can choose to override?"

"Some can, some can't. You'll forgive us if we haven't taken the time to find out the finer points of this computer virus," Cagiao said.

"I would think that would be precisely what you'd be taking the time to do," Janeway snapped. As Cagiao was about to retort, she held up a hand. "I want to hear what's going on in a moment, and I'll offer what aid I can. But first I want to know what has happened to my crewman."

"He's not your crewman any longer, Admiral," Cagiao said. "You don't have a crew."

The comment was not intended to hurt, but Janeway was surprised at how it stung. He was right. She had no crew anymore. They were all scattered, all individuals, each pursuing his own destiny apart from her, apart from *Voyager,* apart from the great adventure they had all shared.

"What did you do?" she said, through clenched teeth.

"He was taken away for questioning," Cagiao said.

"Surely you don't believe he was involved in this," Janeway said.

Cagiao smiled darkly. "It sounds like you came here immediately from your interrupted dinner," he replied. "It would appear that you yourself thought he might be involved."

She did not reply, for he was right. "The Doctor is the author of a holonovel called—"

"*Photons Be Free,* we are quite familiar with it. Which is why a team came by earlier. The Doctor confessed freely to having met with Oliver Baines, and we found on his computer the beginnings of another novel in which the protagonist becomes involved in a holographic revolution."

His voice was still crisp, but his eyes betrayed his sympathy at her surprise. "We also found a padd that Baines left for the Doctor to read. It's chock full of rhetoric about the changing times that lie ahead when photons are finally free, and some of those changes put organics, as they call them, at the bottom and holograms as their masters. Surely you agree there was sufficient cause to take him in for further questioning."

"I don't believe the Doc had any part in this!" Paris said loudly.

Cagiao turned to glare at Tom, and Janeway guessed that Paris was trying his patience. Quickly, she said,

"Tom, answer their questions, and we'll find out what's behind this as soon as possible. That's an order," she said, when he opened his mouth to protest. From another room came a loud wail.

"That's my daughter," Tom said. "Let me go to her."

Cagiao nodded, and Tom was permitted to rise. But a Starfleet security officer accompanied him.

"Commander, it does sound like the Doctor might be able to give you some valuable information about Baines," Janeway said. "But I'm afraid I have to agree with Mr. Paris. I don't think the Doctor would do anything to put human lives in jeopardy."

"They're not, not at the moment at any rate," Cagiao said, "although who knows what kind of riots we'll get once people realize the full extent of this thing."

"May I speak to him?"

Cagiao shook his head. "I'm afraid not, ma'am. Our orders were quite clear."

Janeway set her shoulders. "I outrank you, Mr. Cagiao, and I probably outrank anyone involved in this, so I think you had better—"

"No, ma'am," said Cagiao firmly, "you do not, and as I said my orders were very clear. The Doctor is not allowed to speak to anyone until he is released."

"May I ask the name of the person who issued this order?"

"Admiral Kenneth Montgomery."

AGE FIFTEEN

She is the top student in her class and has already been accepted to Starfleet Academy. She has skipped three years and does not mind leaving her classmates behind each time, as she has never made a real friend in her life.

He wants her to call him Dad, but the owner of the Hand is not her father. And in one of the few acts of rebellion she has ever permitted herself to display, the girl refuses to use the term. He is merely her mother's husband, and she has learned to turn her fear into hatred. It is a powerful shield, hatred, and she does not quite realize that it does as much damage to her soul as her stepfather has done over the years to her body.

Her body has no scars. They are all inside. All the wounds have been turned inward, where they fester like an invisible cancer.

She enters data on her padd, lost in the mathemati-

cal equation, buoyed briefly by a reality that is solid and provable and beyond dispute. It is a rock to cling to in the stormy ocean that is her life, a storm that no one else knows of or can even glimpse.

The door to her bedroom hisses open, and she tenses. Nausea roils inside her. She pretends she does not hear. The owner of the Hand, her mother's husband, comes behind her. She can smell the alcohol on his breath and she shivers. He mistakes her shudder for one of passion. This is not the first time he has come to her room, drunk and swirling with a dark desire.

He reaches for her, groping, hurting. The Hand. She despises the Hand. She imagines herself jumping to her feet, her clothing ripped and the bruises and fluids still evident on her body, screaming for her mother, for justice, for an end to something she knows deep inside is dreadfully wrong, dreadfully evil.

But the words cannot get past the cold lump in her throat, and her body will not move. And the Hands continue their assault.

Chapter

14

It was too bad, Janeway thought as she sat at her computer, that Brian "Red" Grady had been passed over to head Project Full Circle. She knew the jovial, red-haired commander would never have thrown the Doctor in the brig like this. And he was much more pleasant to deal with than Montgomery. But then again, she thought Attila the Hun might be more pleasant to deal with than Montgomery.

"Admiral Montgomery," Janeway said to the handsome but forbidding visage on the screen. "You're a difficult man to get ahold of."

"Apparently not that difficult," he said acerbically. He did not look at all pleased to see her, but she had expected that.

"I understand you're holding the Doctor," she said. "I'd very much like to speak to him."

"That's not possible."

"Of course it's possible, you just don't want me to," she said, blurting out her instinctive response before she could censor herself. "May I ask why?"

"No, actually, it really is not possible," said Montgomery. "The Doctor has been deactivated."

"What?" A chill swept through Janeway. "You haven't deleted his program, have you?"

"Of course not. There's still much valuable information we can get from him in due time. However, he has been deactivated for the present moment."

"You can't do that!"

"Obviously I can and have. Are we to continue playing this little game of semantics, Admiral Janeway, or will you be sensible and let me return to my duties?"

Janeway switched tactics. "You raise an interesting point, Admiral. It was my understanding that you were assigned to Project Full Circle. Chasing down holograms doesn't seem like studying *Voyager*'s unique technology to me. How is the Doctor your problem?"

"He was originally designed to be part of the ship," was the reply. "He was the EMH—Emergency Medical Hologram, in case you've forgotten what the initials stand for. Despite this new technology he sports on his sleeve, the Doctor is as much a part of *Voyager* as any computer console. He, and all other holograms aboard *Voyager,* therefore fall under my purview."

The expression on his face conveyed the truth—he believed what he was saying. The Doctor was nothing more to him than a warp core or a tricorder—just another piece of equipment aboard a ship. What bothered her the most about his attitude was knowing that, not so long ago, she had shared it.

"Why are you detaining him?"

"We have reason to believe that he has been involved in the holographic strike. He has admitted he recognized Baines because he had a little chat with the son of— with him. The Doctor has also been known to stir up trouble with his writing before now."

"Come now, Admiral," Janeway said. "Freedom of speech is one of the Federation's most honored tenets. You're not suggesting censorship?"

"I find it interesting that his sequel deals with a holographic revolution at almost the same time one actually occurs," Montgomery retorted.

"By that logic, all murder-mystery writers would be cold-blooded killers," Janeway replied. "And if you think he was plotting a revolution, do you really believe he'd readily admit that he had ever met Baines?"

She hadn't known about that until Cagiao had informed her, of course, but she trusted the Doctor. She knew he'd learned his lesson with Iden. She hoped that Montgomery hadn't gotten to the ship's logs about that particular incident, but his next words dashed those hopes.

"The Doctor has displayed sympathy for holograms before now," Montgomery said maddeningly. "Certain of your own ship's logs indicate that—"

"If you've read those logs completely, you'll know that the Doctor had nothing to do with the deaths of the

Nuu'bari miners. While he did disobey orders, his intentions were admirable and compassionate. He wanted to protect people he saw as victims from further harm. B'Elanna Torres testified to the Doctor's horror when Iden issued the order to destroy the Nuu'bari vessel."

Anger flashed in the admiral's gray eyes. "He aided renegade holograms at a potentially deadly risk to his own vessel. He was indirectly responsible for—"

And just that quickly, the anger burned itself out. Montgomery sighed, and for a moment looked just like an ordinary, tired man.

"This will get out sooner or later, I suppose, so you might as well know now. While we don't know the full extent of what Baines did to access our systems, we do know of a few key entry sites. And we have recordings and witnesses who can put the Doctor at each of those locations."

Janeway felt the blood drain from her face. "There must be some mistake."

Montgomery shook his fair head and looked almost sorry for her. "No mistake, Admiral. These people swore under oath that he was there, and the recordings show no signs of being tampered with."

"The Doctor has been staying with Lieutenant Commander Paris over the last few weeks, and before that, was with Reginald Barclay," Janeway said.

"You know, I'm willing to bet that neither Paris nor Barclay was watching the Doctor round the clock."

With a sinking feeling, Janeway knew he was right. In fact, Paris had not tried to hide that he deliberately found excuses to leave the Doctor alone. From the little she had been able to get from him during this brief time, the Doctor was playing nursemaid to little Miral, and Tom, like any parent, was taking full advantage of a trusted baby-sitter.

A trusted baby-sitter.... "Did these witnesses see the Doctor carrying a part-Klingon infant?"

Irritated, Montgomery snapped, "Of course not. What nonsense is this?"

"I know that the Doctor was taking care of Lieutenant Commander Paris's daughter. He would never leave an infant unsupervised, especially not his goddaughter."

Montgomery smirked openly. "In light of recent events, I do not share your high opinion of the Doctor's trustworthiness as a nanny, Admiral. Speaking of the Parises, I need to find B'Elanna Torres. I have a great deal of questions that only *Voyager*'s chief engineer would be able to answer. Can you put me in touch with her?"

Janeway narrowed her eyes. "As your security officer so deftly put it, they're not my crew anymore. I have no idea where Lieutenant Torres is. You might want to speak to her husband." Who happened to be standing out of sight behind her, but she wasn't going to do anything to assist this officious man. "You're trying to change the subject, Admiral. I want to speak with the Doctor."

"I told you, he's been—"

"Then reactivate him," Janeway said, a hard edge to her voice.

"He's a security risk if activated."

"Admiral," Janeway said, her voice deceptively calm, "if you reactivate him, all you need to do is place him in a holding cell with holoemitters. If he tries to leave, he'll cease to exist. He's probably the single *most* secure prisoner Starfleet has ever had."

Montgomery said nothing.

"Please let me speak with him," she said, more gently than she had hitherto. "If he's been involved in something like this, he'd be much more likely to be open with me than with you. If he's guilty, I fully agree that he deserves to be punished. But I need to find that out."

Montgomery sighed. "Very well," he said at length. "But your conversation will be monitored."

"Naturally," said Janeway.

"Permission granted. Montgomery out."

It was fortunate, Janeway thought as she was marched down a long corridor with two burly guards on either side, that Starfleet had not gone the way of the civilian sector with regard to the current infatuation with holograms. Many technologies were completely automated. The rest relied on good old humanoids. Janeway felt that while holograms could be programmed to think faster than the human brain, they lacked something unique to humans—intuition and gut instinct.

Even as the thought came to her, she amended it. The Doctor was the exception. He had learned to develop hunches and instinctive responses that had served her and her ship and crew very well indeed over the last few years, but he was unique. He had been active for almost the entire duration of their long, strange journey, and had learned to exceed his programming. Holograms in Starfleet were regulated to entertainment purposes, menial tasks, emergency situations, and extremely dangerous activities so that human lives need not be put at risk. Therefore, while Starfleet itself was scarcely impacted by this peculiar strike, the civilian sector was a huge mess indeed.

She was escorted to an empty cell with a table and two chairs. She glanced up at the corner to see a monitor with a shining red light. Montgomery was indeed going to be recording the conversation.

Several small lights chased each other around the baseboard; then there was a familiar sound and the Doctor stood before her. Delight and relief spread across his familiar face as he reached out to grasp her hands.

"Captain Jane—I mean, Admiral. How very, very good of you to come. I assume I have you to thank for my being reactivated."

She smiled warmly at him, gripping the hands that were nothing more than a forcefield covered by an illusion, but that felt as solid and real as any human hand she'd ever touched.

"I'm only sorry we're seeing each other under these circumstances." She indicated a seat, and as he took it, she pointed to the monitor. He glowered, but nodded his understanding.

"I'm going to do everything I can to see that they don't deactivate you again," she assured him. "And I'm also going to do my utmost to get you legal counsel."

He sighed, slightly dramatically. "I appreciate your efforts, Admiral. But I can't imagine who would be willing to defend a hologram."

She smiled and patted his hand. "Oh, I'll think of

someone. Leave that to me. Now, you have to tell me everything."

Janeway listened intently as the Doctor described Barclay suggesting that he write a sequel to *Photons Be Free,* his distress that no one was thinking to consult him about his remarkable achievements, and how great a balm to his wounded ego Baines's visit had been.

"At least, at first," he amended. "He hid his real purpose for seeing me until he got to the apartment." The Doctor related the conversation. "I was certain I had convinced him that peaceful protest was the only proper means for him to pursue."

"Strikes aren't violent," Janeway pointed out. She filled him in on what had transpired; apparently his captors had not seen fit to do so. "Thus far, nothing dire is happening."

"Other EMHs? Are they striking as well?"

"I've heard nothing about EMHs refusing to render aid," she assured him. He was visibly relieved. "But not many people are going out for dinner these days, and various other processes have come to a screeching halt."

"Well, thank heavens no one's been hurt or killed," said the Doctor.

Janeway hesitated, then said, "I have a bit of bad news."

His eyebrows shot up. *"That* wasn't bad?"

"As I said, so far, nothing serious has happened, but Starfleet feels that if Baines was able to access these systems, he could access others if he isn't found and stopped."

"I agree entirely," said the Doctor. "Baines is quite passionate about the issue of photonic rights. If he doesn't see some movement in that quarter very soon, he may raise the stakes."

"Baines couldn't do all this by himself," said Janeway quietly.

"He did say he had a lot of allies."

"Doctor," she said as gently and compassionately as she could, "you were spotted at several of the break-in sites."

He stared at her. "That's not possible! I've barely left Mr. Paris's apartment. He's quite the taskmaster, and though I adore my goddaughter, I'm frankly a bit weary of playing nursemaid."

"I know," she said, "but the fact is, we have sworn testimony to the fact that you were there. Please—give me something to take back to Admiral Montgomery that can help me get you released."

His dark eyes were thoughtful for a time, and then a dawning comprehension spread across his face. He pounded his fist on the table.

"Baines," he said. "That clever devil."

"Beg your pardon?"

"Admiral, I'm a hologram. I can easily be duplicated, and in fact, Baines had an entire slew of EMH Mark Ones at his disposal."

"Yes," agreed Janeway, "back at the dilithium-processing facility. But you're the only hologram with a personal emitter, Doctor. That technology came from Starling. No one else has it."

The reality of that statement sank in. "But . . . I didn't

do it!" the Doctor said weakly. "Surely you believe me?"

"I do," she assured him. "The trick is going to be getting other people to believe you."

"What about innocent until proven guilty?" said the Doctor angrily. She didn't answer. "It has to be Baines," he said. "He's come up with something, some version of my holoemitter. It's the only explanation. He's an intelligent man, whatever his flaws may be, and he's been the only human surrounded by EMH Mark Ones for several years. He's had ample time to develop something that would help his holograms have freedom of movement."

She smiled sadly. "It is, as Tuvok would say, quite a logical assumption. But until we can get ahold of one of Baines's inventions, you're still the prime suspect. Is there anything else you can tell me?"

The Doctor shook his head sadly. "Thank you for coming, Admiral. It was nice to be activated for at least a little while." He rose, looking resigned. "You may tell the security guards that I'm ready to be deactivated again."

"I'll tell them no such thing," said Janeway. "They've got a cell that's appropriate for you. I'll see what I can do to keep you in it."

He looked suspiciously as if he were going to start crying. "Thank you, Admiral. Thank you."

Tom Paris had barely said a none-too-gracious good-bye to the last security guard when his console beeped. At that precise time, Miral started to cry. He closed his eyes, gathering strength, then rushed to pick up his daughter and see who was trying to get in touch with him.

"Admiral," he said, snapping to attention with such force that Miral was first startled into silence and then threw up on his shoulder.

Admiral Kenneth Montgomery gazed at him and Miral with thinly concealed distaste. "Mr. Paris," he said. "Is Lieutenant Torres available?"

Tom thought about saying something along the lines of *if she was available, either she'd have answered your call or I'd have handed her the shrieking infant,* but decided against it. Miral continued to wail lustily into his right ear.

"I'm afraid not," he said. "Can I take a message?"

"It's difficult to talk to you with your child carrying on like that," Montgomery said.

Paris had to admit he had a point, but bridled at the unnecessary comment nonetheless. "Unfortunately, there's no one here but me to take care of her. B'Elanna's gone and you're holding the Doctor."

Montgomery obviously hadn't missed the dig, but refrained from rising to the bait. "I need to get in touch with her immediately."

"That's not going to be possible, sir. She's on Boreth and I don't know when she'll return." *If ever. God, I miss her.*

"Surely there's some way of contacting her," Montgomery said testily.

"Sir, with respect, she's on leave. What she chooses to do with that time is her business."

Montgomery's expression mutated into one of cold dislike. "Your flip attitude doesn't serve you, Mr. Paris, and I believe it's gotten you into trouble on more than one occasion. If you hadn't been able to hide behind your father, you'd have been in for a lot worse than a short jaunt in a New Zealand penal colony."

Tom felt his face grow hot. "As I said, sir," he said stonily, "B'Elanna is unreachable at the present time."

"That's unfortunate. I'm surprised she was allowed to leave. I have some questions regarding some of *Voyager*'s technology."

"You might try to get in touch with Lieutenant Vorik. I think he's on Vulcan with his family. He was B'Elanna's right hand." Miral's spitup was soaking into his shoulder and growing cold. Tom wanted this conversation to be over.

"Very well, I'll try that. Montgomery out."

For a moment, despite the discomfort of a soggy shoulder, Tom just stood looking at the screen. Miral's screams had subsided into wet snuffly sounds, as they often did when she was held and comforted. Tom took her into the room that served as a nursery, checked her diaper, and then put her in her crib next to her enormous stuffed toy *targ*. She stuck a thumb in her mouth and looked up at her mobile made of tiny models of various Starfleet vessels. Tom changed his shirt, then sat down at the computer.

When Janeway's face appeared, it had a wary look that relaxed into pleasure when she recognized him.

"Hello, Captain. I mean Admiral."

"Has the security team left?"

"Yes, and I just had a little chat with Admiral Montgomery."

"Really? So did I. You go first."

"He wanted to know where B'Elanna was. Permission to speak freely?"

She chuckled. "You're not my helmsman anymore. Speak as freely as you wish."

"I don't like him."

"Well, you're in excellent company and I applaud your taste. I was able to talk to the Doctor."

"Is he okay?"

"He's fine, for now."

Tom was relieved. The whole thing had happened so quickly and so, well, thoroughly that Tom had imagined the worst.

"I even convinced Montgomery to let him stay activated," Janeway continued. "It looks bad for him, Tom. He did talk to Baines, and knew about the plans for a revolution. He says he tried to talk Baines out of it and thought he had succeeded. But it seems he was spotted at many places where this Baines breached security systems and accessed various computers."

"He was baby-sitting!" Tom protested. "He'd never just leave Miral alone like that."

"You know that and I know that, but Montgomery and the other people who are holding the Doctor don't. This holographic strike is really causing a ruckus. They're looking for a scapegoat, and one who isn't human would be ideal."

"We've got to do something," said Tom.

"I agree, and I'm on it. In the meantime," she smiled, "make the most of this precious time alone with your daughter. They grow up so fast."

"Ha ha," said Tom, then closed his mouth with a click. "I'm sorry, Admiral, I didn't mean—"

Janeway waved away his apology. "It's all right, Tom, I was teasing and you teased back. On a more serious note, I hope I may rely on you for assistance should it be needed."

"You can count on it," Tom said.

Chapter

15

"WHOOOOO!" CRIED SEKAYA, tucking up her legs at the last minute to perform a perfect "cannonball" into the lake. While the weapon itself was obsolete, the name for that particular type of dive had lingered. She emerged laughing and gasping, and gazed at her brother with bright eyes. "Dare you!"

Chakotay was moved that she remembered the game they had played as youngsters. Although he had been the one to find this little lake tucked away in the mountains, she had been the first to leap into its welcoming depths. Now he followed her, diving instead of cannonballing, plunging almost to the bottom of the clear, sunlit depths. As he broke the surface, he too was laughing. It felt good to be here.

He had not refused a commission in Starfleet outright, but had chosen to wait to give his answer. He wanted to go home, to the land that had nourished him, to see his family again and swim in the cool sweetness of the lake. As he had known it would, the lengthy visit was slowly but surely restoring his spirit.

He suddenly coughed as Sekaya splashed him. With a mock growl, he struck out after her, but she was swift as an otter and eluded him.

"Slowpoke," she teased. "Guess seven years on a little ship let you get out of shape!"

Sekaya dove deep. The sunlight on the water dazzled Chakotay's eyes, and he lost track of her till she emerged and hopped up onto a large flat rock to let the afternoon sun dry her off.

They were only a year apart in age, and so similar-looking that they could easily be mistaken for twins. Chakotay had been the more "contrary" of the two, but his little sister had also eventually left the shelter of their native land. It was why Chakotay had been able to contact her when he was still back on *Voyager.* The tribe was still as stubborn as ever in its refusal to allow modern technology in the village. Chakotay had had to wait to talk to his mother until he could see her in person.

The night he had arrived, they had a grand feast for him. He stuffed himself silly on roasted fruits, roots, breads, alcohol made from fermented fruit juices. He had danced before the fire as if he had never been away, and slept restfully in the small hut owned by his mother. The sounds of the jungle had been a lullaby. He had had no dreams.

Today, over a month later, he and Sekaya had packed

a picnic lunch and left the village for the day. Their plan had been to return to their old favorite spot. As he lay next to his sister on the rock, both of them silently soaking up the warmth of the sun-warmed stone and the sun itself, he felt the last knot in his soul unravel.

"You haven't said anything about the Borg," Sekaya said, as if reading his mind.

He opened his eyes and looked over at her. She was lying on her stomach, her swimming sarong already dry from the warmth, her head resting on her long brown arms. Her eyes were bright with curiosity.

"You never were one to beat around the bush," grumbled Chakotay.

"Well? You couldn't stop talking about her before."

Chakotay sighed and shut his eyes again, letting the red warmth beat against his closed lids. "Didn't work out."

"Hmm," Sekaya said cryptically. "You going back to Starfleet or staying here? Or neither?"

"Sekky, I don't know," he said. "I came here to get away from those decisions for a while." He'd had enough of soul-searching. The visit to Tevlik's moon with Capt— Admir— dammit, *Kathryn,* had distressed him even more than he thought it would. He wanted quiet, peace, time to just be still.

Time enough for all that in the grave, said a voice. It didn't belong to Sekaya. Chakotay opened his eyes and knew by the strange, dazzling hue of the colors that he had fallen asleep and was having a vivid dream.

Sekaya was gone. In her place, rolling about gleefully in the sun as if it were nothing but an oversized house cat, was an enormous black jaguar.

In the dream state, Chakotay's heart raced. Before, he had encountered Snake and Wolf, even the trickster Coyote a time or two. But Black Jaguar? Jaguar came only rarely, on the eve of events of great import. And Black Jaguar . . . only a few of the most powerful shamans had ever been graced by Her beautiful presence, and none in Chakotay's time. No totem animal had as much *pagata* as Black Jaguar. Chakotay felt every hair on his body stand on end.

He had thought She would be dignified, graceful, elegant. Instead She was undulating on the rock, paws extended to bat the air, and a silly look on Her feline face. As She watched him stare at Her, somewhat disapprovingly, She extended one velvet forepaw, claws carefully sheathed, and delicately patted his face.

You worry too much, Chakotay, he heard Her say in his mind. *You need to lie in the sun on a warm rock now and then.*

I thought that was exactly what I was doing, Chakotay "replied," mildly amused.

Not really. You may look like you're relaxing in the sun, but you're just killing time until you can start fretting again.

Somewhat embarrassed, he realized She was right. *But when I wanted to be still, to be quiet, it sounded like you disapproved.*

You were trying to hide. You weren't embracing a swim and a lie-down in the sun; you were running from your fears. Be active in your relaxing.

Chakotay was thoroughly confused and starting to get annoyed. *I don't understand what you are trying to tell me. First you want me to do something; then you want me to lie in the sun. Coyote is for riddling, not Black Jaguar.*

She rolled upright and stared into his eyes with Her amber ones. Chakotay tasted fear, coppery and cold, in his throat. Black Jaguar was not to be trifled with, even if She did just look like a big cat who'd found some particularly potent catnip.

What is Black Jaguar for, then, little human?

He had displeased Her, he knew it. He took a deep breath, and recited what the shamans had said. *Black Jaguar is the totem of great power, of courage, of ferocity. Of fighting great battles in just causes. Of dealing out death to those who deserve it, and not flinching from the task. Black Jaguar strikes without warning and kills swiftly and fairly. When Black Jaguar appears, one is about to . . . .*

He found he couldn't even dare to think the words. Black Jaguar finished the homily for him.

One is about to embark on a journey that will test one's mettle, wits, courage, and faith in the dark places. It is a trial of the highest sort, and if one fails, then Black Jaguar will exact Her punishment. And if one succeeds, great good will come about, for the journeyer and the world.

Chakotay stared at Her, his heart cold in his chest. She met his gaze evenly, then flopped back on Her warm rock. *Now do you see why you ought to fully live the moment, Chakotay? With so much ahead of you, you'd better take your sun-moments where you can.*

"Chakotay." He stirred. "Chakotay, wake up. You were talking in your sleep."

He opened his eyes to see Sekaya's concerned face peering down at him. Bolting upright, he looked around frantically. There was, of course, no sign of Black Jaguar. She lived in the Spirit World, not here.

"What are you looking for?"

"Nothing," he said, "just the remnants of a dream." He turned to her and grinned, doing his utmost to fully and truly embrace Black Jaguar's last words. He knew that it was time to return to the world he had temporarily left behind.

"Hey," he said. "I'm hungry. Let's go find some pineapple."

Chakotay figured he probably shouldn't do this.

In fact, he was certain that he shouldn't. But the words, if one could call them that, of Black Jaguar echoed in his mind. He needed to *live,* not brood and ponder and hide and think. So after saying farewell to his tranquil mother and his lively, vibrant sister, Chakotay returned to San Francisco. There was always a friend or two he could look up, and maybe Kathryn might want to get together for dinner as they once did. While having coffee with his old friend Sveta, he asked if he could use the computer. She arched an eyebrow and he had to laugh. Sveta knew, of course, whom he wanted to talk to.

"Sure that's such a good idea? Sounded like she didn't want to hear from you, from what I saw at the banquet."

"No, I'm not sure it's a good idea," replied Chakotay. "But it's what I want to do. She needs to know that just because we're not involved or interacting on a daily basis doesn't mean I don't want to continue being her friend. I liked and respected her before we became . . . before. I still do."

"You are the only man I know of who can really say that and mean it," said Sveta admiringly. "I hope she accepts the olive branch. Your friendship is something to be cherished, Chakotay."

He extended a hand and she clasped it; then she left him alone and went to brew another pot of coffee. He sat down at her desk and took a deep breath, then gave the computer the proper instructions.

Irene Hansen's cheerful, wrinkled face appeared on the screen. Before he could introduce himself, she chuckled.

"We haven't had the pleasure of meeting, Commander Chakotay, but I knew I'd know that tattoo when I saw it. How are you, young man?"

Any anxiety he had been feeling abated in front of that comfortable smile. "Very well, Ms. Hansen. And how are you?"

"Glorious!" she enthused. "The weather's lovely and I'm making strawberry shortcake. Maybe you can stop over and have a bite. Got some real cream to whip too."

"That's very kind of you. Perhaps I'll take you up on that; it sounds delicious. May I speak to Seven?"

"Just a minute." Irene disappeared from the viewscreen. "Annika, honey, that nice Chakotay wants to talk to you."

Chakotay couldn't help himself. He started laughing.

He was still laughing when Seven's beautiful face appeared on the screen. Her eyes were bright and her lips were parted in a smile.

"I apologize for my aunt," she said, and even as she spoke he saw the cool mask slip down over the face of the laughing girl.

Anxious to recapture the moment, Chakotay said, "Don't. She is, as they used to say, quite a card. I like her."

Seven smiled, fleetingly, shyly. "I do as well. How are you faring?"

"I'm all right. I wanted to see how you were adjusting."

She seemed to ponder the question. "I am well. Aunt Irene has been . . . ." She hesitated, groping for the word.

"Fun?"

She smiled. "Yes. She has been fun. I have been acquiring new skills, such as preparing foodstuffs and repairing defective items."

"You mean, learning how to cook and fix things around the house."

"I believe I said precisely that."

He looked at her and saw a twinkle in her eye and realized with surprise that she was teasing him. He was delighted. It seemed as though this genial aunt was a profoundly humanizing influence. Perhaps she'd been right, after all. Perhaps she needed to learn from others, strike out on her own, to develop her human personality. Who was Seven of Nine when she was on Earth? They both needed to know that, and the only way to discover it was for her to do exactly what she was doing.

"You were starting to become a pretty good chef yourself back on *Voyager*," he reminded her. "I'm sure you have some recipes to share with your aunt."

"She excels at baking, a skill I have yet to acquire. But you are correct. We have been learning from one another."

"It's good to see you," he said honestly. "I'm so pleased to hear you're doing so well."

Her smile faltered.

"Not so well?"

She hesitated, then said, "I am glad to be able to talk to you. There is something happening that puzzles me."

"Go on."

"Recently I have been experiencing a sensation of—"

In the distance, Chakotay heard noises. He caught a few words uttered in a deep male voice: "Starfleet order . . . don't interfere . . . please, ma'am . . ." and Irene's responses: "proper authorization . . . wait, you can't go in there. . . ."

Seven's blond head whipped around and he saw her stiffen, saw her almost physically don the armor that had helped her to "adapt" to life among humans. "Who's there?"

"Seven, what's going on?" Chakotay asked, hearing his own voice deepen and adopt the timbre of command.

She rose, not responding, and he could see only her long, slim torso as she turned to face whoever had entered the room. "This is a private home," she stated. "What is your authorization to enter?"

"Please don't resist," came a voice. "We just want you to come in for questioning."

"Questioning? About what?" Seven's voice was haughty.

"This is Commander Chakotay. What's going on?"

A face appeared in front of the screen. For a moment, Chakotay stared into the green eyes of a grim-faced man dressed in Starfleet mustard, gray, and black. Then the screen went dark.

Chakotay swore, something he did not often do, and immediately put in a call to Kathryn. Her face, when it appeared on the screen, was as angry as he had ever seen it.

"So you know," he said without preamble.

"I do," she replied grimly. "They can't hold him for long, though. At least I hope not. I'm trying—"

"Him?" Chakotay exclaimed. "Starfleet just barged into Irene Hansen's house and arrested Seven of Nine."

Now it was her turn to stare. "Seven? What the— For the last two days I've been pulling every string I can think of to get the Doctor released. He's been taken in for questioning about this hologram strike. Surely they don't think Seven was connected with this?"

"I don't know what they think. I only know they've taken her."

"I'll get right on it. Where can I contact you?"

"Give me two minutes and I'll be right there with you—if that's all right."

"Better than all right," she replied promptly. Her face was set in a defiant expression that was quite familiar to him. "I feel sorry for anyone having to deal with the two of us when we've got our dander up."

Despite the direness of the situation, he grinned. The

smile faded as her image did, and his thoughts turned to his vision of Black Jaguar.

Her appearance betokened a journey into darkness, a trial both powerful and frightening. Disaster awaited failure, but great good would come about with success.

He wished he'd had another day or two of lying on a sun-warmed rock.

When Sam, Tim, and Andre fell into step beside Icheb, he smiled happily.

"Hey guys, how's it going?" He was pleased with himself for remembering the casual phrase so often used as a greeting among the cadets. It was one of many things he'd had to learn as part of his adaptation to life as a Starfleet Academy student.

The four of them and Eshe had become almost inseparable. Over the last month they ate out together, studied together, and would have roomed together if they'd been able to. Icheb had never really had any friends to speak of. Naomi came close, but although she was highly intelligent for her age, she was still emotionally much younger than he. Seven was a friend of a sort, but more of a big sister. These were his compatriots and confidants. Finally, he belonged.

With Eshe, the relationship was starting to become more than friendship. Only the day before yesterday, when they said good night after an evening of studying, she had reached up to him, stroked his pale cheek with her dark hand, and brought her lips to his. The sensation was new but quite pleasant. She pulled away and smiled up at him, and then it was his turn to reach for her.

His friends remained silent. Icheb recalled a pastime that was popular among cadets and introduced the subject. "Does anyone wish to consume pizza this—"

He paused in midsentence, looking at the expressions on the faces around him, his certainty as to the appropriateness of his comments faltering. That had been one of the hardest things for him to learn. As a Borg, there had been no need to communicate through facial expressions or tone of voice. All was known, all was shared. He had had to learn that upturned lips on nearly every humanoid species meant pleasure, that water coming from the eyes meant distress, that drawn-together eyebrows meant anger. Now he looked from one of his friends to the other, trying to decipher their emotions.

They had come to a halt beside a small copse of trees on the ground. Eshe now stepped out from behind one. Icheb looked at her curiously. Her eyes were red and her face was more serious than he had ever seen it.

"Icheb," she said, her voice flat, "you have to answer some questions."

"I do not understand," he said. "What is it you wish to know?"

Tim snorted. His face was flushed and his breathing was heavy. It distressed Icheb when those he cared about were troubled. Tim was the weakest student among them; perhaps he was not doing well in a class.

"Like you don't know," he snarled.

"Truly, Tim, I do not."

Eshe sighed. "Maybe he really doesn't, Tim."

Tim looked away. "Of course he does. He's got to. My dad got a message today." His voice was as flat as Eshe's. "I wasn't supposed to know about it. No one is, but he can't keep something like this quiet forever. So I heard all about it. *Borg.*"

The way he said the last word unsettled Icheb. "That is an incorrect term, Tim. You know I am no longer a member of the collective."

"Icheb," said Eshe, "listen. We've—we've heard something. We want to know what you have to do with it."

"With what?" Icheb asked. He stumbled forward suddenly. Andre had shoved him! Icheb whirled, staring at his friend's face. "Andre, why did you do that?"

"My aunt was killed at Wolf 359, you bastard!" Andre cried. His voice was thick and Icheb realized his friend was crying. He was so surprised at the unprovoked attack and so focused on Andre's lean, tear-streaked face that he didn't see Sam's fist coming. The blow to his head took him completely off-guard, and he fell forward onto the walkway, his padds clattering as they tumbled out of his pack.

"What are you doing?" came Eshe's voice. "We were just going to question him!"

Tim reached down and grabbed onto Icheb's shirt, but by now Icheb was aware of what was happening, although he didn't understand why and it pained him deeply. He had spoken truly; he was no longer a member of the collective, but the implants that remained in his body made him stronger and swifter than any of his three colleagues, and his senses were heightened.

With shocking speed he struck at Tim's arm, knocking his grip loose. Icheb ducked Sam's blow and dealt one of his own. Andre grabbed him from behind and before Icheb could extricate himself, Tim had landed a good punch to his midsection.

Icheb gasped in pain. Another blow crashed down on his face and he tasted blood. He dropped to his knees, reaching behind him and seizing Andre in the same movement. With effort, for he was winded and hurt, he flung Andre over his head. Andre hit the pavement hard and went limp.

Concern for his friend made Icheb hesitate. Sam rushed over to Andre.

"Okay," said Sam, breathing heavily. "Okay, this is enough. Andre needs some help." Sam looked over at Icheb. "Icheb, we—"

Tim fell upon Icheb, raining blows. He felt something hard strike him and realized that Tim had grabbed ahold of some of the rocks that artfully dotted the landscape and was using these as well. Instinctively, Icheb covered his head.

What was going on? Why were they attacking him so? Had there been a Borg attack? Surely everyone would have heard about it. He would have been contacted by Seven, by Starfleet. He could have helped them fight the dreadful foe that all of them despised.

Blows rained down upon him, and he felt a kick to his midsection. Eshe cried, "Stop it, you're killing him!" and Icheb was vaguely aware that Sam was trying to pull an enraged Tim off him. Everyone was yelling, and for some reason, Icheb wasn't feeling the pain of the blows as much. It was as if he were floating away. Tim landed a kick to his groin, and after the exquisite flash of white-hot agony, the world around Icheb started to go gray.

Although physically he was ceasing to feel the beating, intellectually he knew that Tim wasn't letting up even though he felt himself start to go limp. He wasn't fighting back anymore, was offering no resistance. A phrase flickered through his brain, and even at this awful moment he found it humorously ironic: *Resistance is futile.*

It was at that moment that he understood that unless Eshe and Sam succeeded in pulling Tim off him, Tim would continue striking him after he lost consciousness, after he was no longer a physical threat, and that it was entirely possible that Tim would continue to beat him until Icheb was dead. The knowledge hurt worse than the physical attack.

Abruptly, the shower of blows stopped. Icheb's face was so swollen he could barely open his eyes. He struggled to do so, and when he did, he saw blue sky and clouds. Then a face appeared in his vision—a dark face, with brown eyes and pointed ears.

Tuvok lifted him easily, and Icheb knew no more.

Chapter
16

SEVEN WENT ALONG QUIETLY, though anger and confusion smoldered inside her. She feared for her aunt's safety if she failed to comply and knew that it would not take long for Admiral Janeway to hear about the incident. Seven had done absolutely nothing wrong, and despite repeated queries, none of the guards would tell her what she was charged with. She had stayed at Irene Hansen's house from the moment she arrived home. Whatever she was accused of, it was false, and surely she would be released soon.

She held her fair head high as they marched her down a corridor to a holding cell. She paid no attention to the other prisoners, but heard a gasp and a cry of "Seven!" Turning, she was startled to see the Doctor imprisoned in a cell across the corridor.

"You two know each other?" one of the guards said. "Well, you'll have plenty of time to chat." He keyed in a code and the forcefield dropped. Seven stepped inside. There was a hum as the field was reactivated. The two guards left.

"Seven, what's happened?" the Doctor cried. "Why are you in prison?"

"I do not know. They will not tell me what I am accused of. What are the charges you face?"

"I'm not sure what exactly, but they think I'm somehow connected with the holographic uprising."

Seven arched a blond eyebrow. "Are you?"

"Of course not!" he huffed. He glanced away from her, though, as he added, "I did speak to the ringleader, I admitted as much. And I was working on a holonovel based on a holographic revolution, but it was purely a work of fiction. I am beginning to think that Starfleet and the Federation have changed a great deal from the institutions with which we are familiar."

"I am utterly unfamiliar with them, and had I known what awaited me I believe I might have left *Voyager* before it returned to Federation space."

"A sentiment I'm beginning to share," said the Doctor. "I've spoken with Admiral Janeway. I'm sure she's doing everything she can to—"

Seven followed his shocked gaze and realized why he had stopped in midsentence.

When she saw Icheb shuffling slowly toward her prison cell, two armed guards poking him in the back, Seven couldn't completely stifle a cry of alarm. He ran to her and she hugged him, then stepped back to stare at his swollen face. Fury raged in her and she whirled on the guards.

"He is only an adolescent boy," she cried. "Was it necessary to enact such violence upon him?"

The guards bridled and started to speak, but Icheb spoke first. "Seven, they didn't hurt me."

"Then who did?"

He looked away, unable to meet her fierce, protective gaze. "Some cadets at the Academy. They said something about me being Borg."

"The boy requires medical assistance," the Doctor snapped. "You should have attended to his injuries first."

"There was nothing life-threatening," said one of the guards. "Don't worry, you'll both be seeing the doctor here soon." Without further comment, they stepped outside and the forcefield crackled as it snapped back into place.

"What happened, Icheb?" asked Seven. "Please explain."

Slowly, haltingly, Icheb recounted the incident. Seven and the Doctor listened without interrupting. She pressed him on the Borg comments, but Icheb could recall nothing of substance. Seven latched on to the one thing that might provide enlightenment.

"Tim said something about overhearing a message his father received," she said. "What is his father's occupation?"

"I do not know for certain," Icheb said. His voice was slurred because of his swollen mouth. Seven again felt a rush of anger. It was uncharacteristically cruel of Starfleet security not to have treated Icheb's wounds.

There might not be anything life-threatening, but he was deliberately being permitted to suffer, and it infuriated her.

"Tim has never been allowed to tell us much. His father works for Starfleet security, possibly on a very high level. It could be that he received information about a Borg attack that has not yet been made public."

Seven had come to the same conclusion, but it made little sense to her. If there had been a Borg attack, the expedient course would be to immediately mount a counterattack. Nothing would be gained by keeping such knowledge secret and not acting upon it. That was a certain path to assimilation. But if the Borg were somehow involved, she suddenly knew why she had been accosted in her own home, forcibly and probably illegally removed, and why frightened cadets would turn so viciously on a friend. Fear of the Borg was a dreadful thing, and unfortunately, a logical response to a profoundly dangerous threat.

She changed the subject as she examined his face. "The security guards were correct, though it was hardly a qualified medical assessment," she said. "I do not believe that you are damaged beyond repair."

His bruised mouth curved into a smile at her choice of words, and almost at once he winced from the pain. Seven felt a pang, but did not change her expression. It would not assist Icheb to display excessive pity for his condition.

"The body's not what hurts so bad," he said softly, barely loud enough for her to hear.

She knew exactly what he meant. "It is difficult

when those we have come to care for appear to have turned against us," she said. It was not fair for Icheb to have to have suffered this even once, let alone twice in his short lifetime. First his parents had betrayed him, and now his youthful colleagues had physically damaged him.

"Do you think they'll let us go?" he asked.

"I have insufficient data to predict their response," Seven replied. "I was, however, in communication with Commander Chakotay at the precise time that security came to Aunt Irene's house. It is likely he will attempt to intervene on our behalf."

"And Admiral Janeway knows about my situation, at least," added the Doctor. "I'm sure she'll find out about you two as well."

"Commander Tuvok stopped the—" Icheb obviously couldn't bring himself to say the negative words "attack" or "beating," so he said no word at all. "He stopped it, so I know he knew what was happening."

"So, Commanders Tuvok and Chakotay are aware of the situation. It is likely that they will notify Admiral Janeway. Do not get too comfortable, Icheb," she said, attempting to tease. "I do not think we will be here for much longer." She looked over at the Doctor, expecting a witty confirmation of her statement, but he said nothing. And she saw doubt in his dark holographic eyes.

Icheb was permitted to see the doctor first. He returned looking whole and healthy once more, his injuries healed. But the way he carried himself communicated to Seven that the wounds he had incurred at the hands of his new collective of cadets had gone far deeper than mere damage to his flesh. Outrage flashed through her as she thought about it. Starfleet cadets were supposed to be the finest representatives of their generation. They were supposed to be tolerant, compassionate, protective of the weak. And yet, how viciously they had turned on their own at the mere thought of a Borg threat.

She still had not been told why she and Icheb had been incarcerated. They were treated well enough, and she was more pleased and moved than she wanted to admit that they were able to talk with the Doctor. Seven knew she had to present a strong, confident front for Icheb's sake as well as her own. He was watching her now more intently than ever he had before, and she needed to do all she could to reassure him. Having the Doctor to talk to helped her to maintain her proud, fearless façade, and she was grateful.

One of the guards approached and deactivated the forcefield. "Please come with me," he said.

"Where are we going?"

"You're to see Dr. Kaz."

She glanced back at Icheb, who gave her the first hint of a smile that she had gotten from him since the entire absurd and unjust affair began, and went quietly.

Dr. Jarem Kaz was a Trill. He turned to look at her with large, friendly blue eyes and a smile that appeared genuine. He was tall and well built, approaching middle age. His spots were quite dark and were clustered closer to the hairline than was usual with his species.

"Please, come in and sit down," he said. Seven eyed

him, trying to take his measure. Since Icheb had given her a reassuring smile while she was being led to see him, Kaz was therefore someone she was inclined not to negatively prejudge.

Her initial positive impression of him was further heightened when he turned brusquely to the lingering guard and said, "Thank you, that will do. I'll take care of her," and all but pushed him out the door. When the door hissed closed behind the guard, Kaz sighed and shook his head. He turned back to Seven.

"I'm Dr. Jarem Kaz," he said.

She didn't answer.

"You aren't monitored here," he said. "Not that I expect you to speak freely, but I wanted you to know."

Seven lifted a golden eyebrow. "Thank you," she said stiffly.

"I must apologize for the red tape that kept Icheb in pain for so long," he said, picking up a medical tricorder and beginning to scan her. "There's no excuse for that. I've recommended that he be allowed to speak to a counselor if he chooses. I understand that the people who beat him so badly were fellow Starfleet cadets."

Seven said nothing to confirm or deny his statement. He paused, as if waiting for her to speak, then continued.

"Bad business, that. Fear makes people do cruel things, things they'll be ashamed of later."

"Such as bringing in Federation citizens and holding them without charges or counsel," said Seven.

Kaz nodded and sighed again. "Such as that," he agreed. "Well, if I keep running my mouth, then they'll probably toss me in with you."

She looked at him hard. "Is that truly a possibility?" she inquired.

He laughed. "No, I'm just teasing you." He looked at his tricorder and frowned. "It appears your ocular implant is out of alignment."

He approached with a tool but she ducked back. "How do you know how to correct it?" she demanded.

"I've read everything the Doctor has reported on you and Icheb," he said. "I've only just finished, which is one of the reasons I'm unforgivably late in seeing you. I should have been allowed to see Icheb sooner, though; his injuries had nothing to do with his being Borg."

"He is no longer part of the collective," Seven said, "and neither am I."

"I understand the difference," said Dr. Kaz. "I won't try to adjust this if you don't want me to. The misalignment is minor and it's not a vital implant."

Seven thought about it. Jarem Kaz struck her as a good person, better than she had expected. Only the Doctor had actual experience adjusting her implants, so even with someone she trusted, it would be a risk. She did not think that Kaz would attempt to harm her in any way, and even if he did, she would be able to react before he did any lasting damage.

"You may proceed," she said at length.

"Thank you," he said, and began his adjustment.

"Perhaps this will eliminate the unusual sensations I have been experiencing," said Seven.

"What kind of sensations?"

"It is a slight hum," she said. "Almost like voices, but not quite."

Kaz froze for an instant, then continued. "Is it anything like you experienced when you were joined with the collective?"

"No," said Seven promptly. "We were linked clearly to the hive mind. There was no confusion whatsoever. If there was any attempt by the Queen to give instructions they were, as a friend of mine would say, crystal clear. This is much fainter, much more incoherent."

"Do you think someone might be trying to activate your implants?"

Suddenly realizing what he was asking, Seven grabbed his wrist.

"Seven, you're hurting me," said Kaz quietly, making no attempt to free himself.

She loosened her viselike grip but did not release him. "Why are you asking such questions?"

"You told me you were getting some kind of reception with your implants," he said. "I was merely theorizing."

"There is something going on with the Borg," said Seven, knowing she should wait until she had legal counsel, but also suspecting that that might take a long time. "This is why Icheb and I were brought here. Tell me what is transpiring. I have no cause to love the Borg, Dr. Kaz. My loyalties lie with Admiral Janeway and what she represents. I would be pleased to assist, but I resent being thrown into prison without even knowing what I am accused of."

"Let me go, Seven," said Kaz. She did so, and he took a step back, rubbing his reddening arm. "You understand that I am bound by orders," he said.

"I do," Seven replied.

"I have determined from examining you that you are not . . . not what they think. That you are not *doing* what they think, nor is Icheb. I will do what I can to release you. But you're going to have to assist me in return."

"How?"

"I will tell the guards that you are not well and that your situation needs monitoring. That any time you wish to see me, day or night, you must be allowed to do so. And I want you to promise that you'll come talk to me if anything changes with your implants."

She eyed him. "You will be forced to tell them what you know," she said.

"I will," he said. "But the more I know about what's going on with you, the more I can help you."

"Why do you want to help me?"

"I told you. I've just examined you and I know that you're innocent of . . . what they suspect. I wish I could say more, but I have my orders, as I have said. I know I'm asking you to trust me based on nothing, and it's your call."

Seven reached to touch her facial implant. "You have not corrected the problem," she said, slightly accusingly.

"I have indeed realigned your implant," he said, "but it would seem that's not what's causing the problem."

She was silent; then she rose. "If you have completed your exam, I should return to my cell."

His blue eyes searched hers. Finally he said, "Very well. I will call your guard. Remember what I've told you, and be careful what you say and whom you trust."

* * *

Seven assumed that the two guards would escort her back to her cell. Instead, they took her to a turbolift, which, after a long interval, opened directly into a small, dark room. Seven threw her shoulders back. She knew what was about to happen.

One of the guards prodded her with a phaser. She stepped forward. Immediately the doors hissed closed behind her. She was in utter darkness.

"Seven of Nine," came a cool male voice in the darkness. "I imagine you know what you're here for."

"I am here to be interrogated," she said, keeping her voice as cool and unemotional as that of the stranger in the dark room.

"And why do you think that is?"

"I have no idea. I submitted to a full debriefing when *Voyager* returned to Federation space. I will be amenable to answering fully and honestly any questions you have for me, despite the fact that you are holding me with no charges." She lifted her chin, although it was too dark for anyone to see the defiant gesture. "I have nothing to hide."

"Brave words. But I think they're lies. I think you know something you're not telling. And I think I know how to get that information out of you."

Hands came out of the darkness. Several of them, all strong. Seven struggled instinctively but they overcame her. She was shoved into a chair. She heard a clang and felt metal close about her body, leaving only her head free.

"If you do not resist," came another voice, this one soft and feminine, "this will not hurt. I have no desire to cause you pain."

Out of the darkness came the touch of fingers, curiously warm and gentle. They positioned themselves on her skull. Her mind slid open like a door and she felt the Vulcan's presence inside.

"And of course," said the first voice, chuckling a little, "we all know that resistance is futile. Don't we, Borg?"

The Vulcan dove deeper into her mind. As if from a great distance, Seven heard the Vulcan's emotionless voice recite details from Seven's life as if reading from a not-very-interesting report.

After a time, the interrogator probed more deeply, into things Seven did not wish to share with strangers, and she felt the first few flickers of pain.

And when the Vulcan began to speak about the ravens, Seven started to scream.

Little Kevin Johnson whimpered in his sleep. Above him, a small mobile revolved, emitting soft nursery music. Inside his crib, the toddler tossed and turned. Beneath tightly shut lids, his eyes darted back and forth. His cheeks flushed, then paled, then flushed again. But he did not awaken.

Inside his body, racing along his veins, something alien went about its programmed duty. Microscopically tiny, perfectly constructed machines came to life, replicated, latched on to blood cells. With each passing second, more and more of them appeared and began systematically replacing human anatomy with machine.

And on his soft, fragile baby's cheek, a spidery Borg implant erupted.

Chapter

17

JANEWAY WAS EXHAUSTED when she returned to her small apartment. Things had happened so fast. First the Doctor had been arrested, and now Seven and Icheb were in prison. Seven looked tense and strained when Janeway and Tuvok finally got permission to see her, but everything she said was clearly meant to put their minds at ease. It was Tuvok who noticed that there was no regeneration chamber available for either former Borg, and went to speak with one of the guards.

Janeway wasn't too concerned about Seven. She'd demonstrated that she could go for several days without regenerating. Icheb was a different matter. Janeway was worried about more than the lack of a regeneration chamber for the young man. Icheb was quite silent and seemed troubled. Once she learned what had happened to the youth, Janeway shared Seven's outrage. She had bent the ears, or perhaps a better word would be "blistered," of several important personages in the Federation already and had messages in to several more.

She'd also arranged for Chakotay to meet with Seven at some point. He had told her that Seven had called off their relationship so that she might better learn who she was here on Earth. Apparently, who she was here on Earth was a mistreated prisoner. She might welcome a visit from a friend who was once something more.

A soft sound from her computer almost as soon as she entered the room made her groan aloud. Who could it be now? It was almost three in the morning. Sighing, she eased into her chair. "On screen," she said.

Carla Johnson's tear-streaked, large-eyed face filled the screen. Before Janeway could speak, she cried, "What did you do to him?"

"Carla? What's going on? What's happened?"

"Kevin," Carla said, sobbing now. "Kathryn, what did you do to him? Oh, my God, my God . . . ."

She turned away from the screen as Mark stuck his face in. He too looked dreadfully upset, but was trying to be calm.

"Mark, what's going on? Is Kevin all right?"

"No, he's not. He's . . . we assumed that because of *Voyager* . . . ?" Mark cleared his throat. "We've contacted the authorities and they're on their way, but we wanted to talk to you first, to see if you knew what— We know you wouldn't do anything deliberately to hurt him, but . . . ." Mark's voice trailed off.

"Mark," said Janeway calmly, though her heart was

racing, "take a deep breath and tell me clearly. What is going on? Is Kevin ill?"

"Look at him!" Carla cried, thrusting Kevin toward the screen.

Janeway gasped, the hair on her arms standing on end in horror. Kevin was strangely silent for such a young child, and he stared at Janeway blankly. His skin was an ashen shade of gray, and strange veins crawled over his small body like insects. One eye didn't seem quite right to her and—

Her hand went to her mouth. "I'll be right—"

The screen went dark.

To his credit and to Janeway's enormous relief, Chakotay didn't bat an eye at being asked to bring his little *Alpha Flyer* out for a jaunt at three in the morning. They arrived at the Johnsons' house in Colorado shortly after he picked her up, and Janeway barely waited for the shuttlecraft to fully settle before opening the door and jumping out. She raced to the front stoop of the Johnsons' pleasant little home and knocked frantically. There was no answer, not even Molly's loud barking.

"Looks like nobody's home," Chakotay said, stepping beside her.

"That's just not possible," Janeway said, more to herself than to Chakotay. She hadn't told him what she'd seen, only that her friends needed her immediately because their child was desperately ill.

"They said Kevin was sick," Chakotay continued. "Maybe they took him to a doctor. He could have that flu that's been going around."

Janeway went cold inside. "Xakarian flu," she repeated. "Symptoms are cold skin, paleness, delusions . . . oh my God."

"Kathryn, what is it?"

She wanted to tell him, but she couldn't, not until she knew for sure. "Take me home," she said, and though he looked at her quizzically, he obliged.

"What the hell have you done with the Johnsons?" she cried as soon as Montgomery's face appeared on her computer screen.

He stared at her. He had thrown on a robe and his fair hair stuck up at odd angles. He obviously wanted to be deeply angry but couldn't seem to summon the energy.

"Kathryn, it's nearly four in the morning."

"I'm well aware of what time it is. I have to tell you that I am getting tired of people I care about disappearing with no explanations. Let me ask you again: What happened to the Johnsons?"

"Who are you talking about, and what makes you think I know anything about these people?"

She narrowed her eyes. "Two words: Xakarian flu."

"If they were suspected of having contracted it, they have to be quarantined. If you have a problem with that, you'll need to take that up with Starfleet Medical. That's not my field." He extended a hand as if to terminate the conversation.

"You're conducting a cover-up," Janeway said.

That stopped him. "Of what?"

"I saw Kevin. I saw the implants. How convenient

that Xakarian flu has all the symptoms of the early stages of Borg infection."

Montgomery stiffened visibly, and was suddenly very wide awake. "I'm sorry you saw that. We wanted to do this quietly, to avoid panic, but your sniffing around has forced my hand. I'm going to have to call everyone who served aboard *Voyager* in for questioning. Starting with her captain."

Gray Bear looked at the strained face of James Red Feather. James had been the medicine man who had instructed Gray Bear, but now he was on the receiving end of the healing medicine he had once given of so freely. His face was haggard and drawn, the wrinkles looking as if they were physically cut into his aged face. The sickness had come upon him suddenly, a mere two days ago, and Gray Bear had had to make haste to gather people and materials for the sweat lodge. He feared to wait another day. Federation medicine was available for the asking, of course, and immediately after the sweat lodge he would take James to the doctor. But the lodge always came first. Healing took place on many levels.

It was a full lodge today. James was well loved and many had been more than happy to attend, to lend their voices to the singing and chanting that would help heal their fellow tribe member and respected elder. The Sioux believed that facing up to the intense heat and darkness of the lodge would purge all those who attended, especially the sick one in whose name the sweat lodge had been called.

There was a hissing sound as Gray Bear poured another dipperful of water on the stones. The steam rose, twining about them, ready to begin purifying both body and spirit. The women were on one side, clad in pure cotton clothing, their arms and legs modestly covered. The men sat on the other side, their bodies bare to the waist. There was no jewelry on anyone present—the spirits disliked jewelry, and besides, metal would become hot enough to burn mere human skin in the lodge.

Gray Bear's apprentice poked his head into the circular opening. Gray Bear nodded. The apprentice closed the deerskin flap and proceeded to seal it tight. There were a few pinpricks of light, but those were quickly covered up. Utter blackness descended. Blackness, and moisture, and healing, almost unbearable, heat.

During the nearly four hours of the ritual, no one would be permitted to leave. It would weaken the medicine. There would be four "doors" in today's ceremony, four times when the flap would be lifted and cool air and bright light would waft in to revive those who huddled in the darkness. But all were expected to remain inside the lodge for the duration of the ceremony.

Gray Bear began to chant, a call-and-response chant in his native tongue. The answers were firm and clear. Then there was silence for a time. He sat erect and tall in the darkness, feeling the sweat pour off his body like rainwater sluicing down his skin. Now and then, he would reach for the dipper and pour more water on the hot coals. Their red, pulsating glow was the only thing visible in the entire lodge.

He heard the sounds of people shifting, moving their bodies and faces down toward the cool earth. Some pressed their noses to the place where tent met soil, breathing the cool air. There was no shame in this. One participated as much as one could, and some could withstand the excruciating, stifling heat better than others.

Time passed in that timeless place. Deep silence descended.

And then there was the scream.

It took Gray Bear a few precious seconds to realize that the sound came from the throat of James Red Feather, and by then other screams had joined it. The tent remained closed; the apprentice knew that sometimes participants had visions, and would not open the flap unless explicitly told to do so.

"Be calm!" Gray Bear called out. "The spirits are with us!" Even as he spoke, he knew it was a lie. There had never been a spirit visitation that had afflicted so many, and Gray Bear's sharp ears detected the subtle differences between the cries of ecstatic delight and fear and those of pain and real, present terror.

He made his decision. "Open the flap!" he cried. "Open it, open it!"

The flap was opened. Daylight poured into the lodge and there was a mad scramble for the door. Gray Bear stared in horror at James Red Feather. He was writhing and screaming, tearing at his own flesh. The sunlight glinted on metal sprouting from his body as if it was growing there, and even as James tried to pull it out, his hands blistered as they touched it. He turned to look at Gray Bear, and his eyes were dead and cold.

Suddenly James stiffened. He turned swiftly and, with two thin tubes that had erupted from his flesh, jabbed a woman frantically trying to escape.

"Resistance is futile," said James in Sioux. He swiveled his head and impaled Gray Bear with his evil gaze, and then methodically approached, his arm with its awful tubes extended.

And then it was the medicine man's turn to scream.

Tom Paris opened the door and sighed when he saw who was standing there.

"You know, you guys really ought to give a fellow warning," he said, stepping back and grandly sweeping his arms to invite Starfleet Security inside. "I'd have replicated some tea and cookies for you. In the meantime, I do have a pot of hot coffee at the ready. It's been a long night."

Their faces were as impassive as Tuvok's. No wonder the Vulcan had been such a great security chief; apparently a poker face was part of the uniform.

"We're going to have to ask you to come with us, Lieutenant Commander," one of them said.

"Not this again," Paris said, his voice rising. Miral was having a bad bout of colic tonight, and he was irascible and exhausted from sitting up with her. "I've answered all your questions and you've got the Doc himself in custody."

"This isn't about the HoloStrike, sir," the commanding officer said. They had sent out a new batch, Tom observed. He didn't recognize any of the men standing in his apartment.

"What *is* it about?"

"I'm afraid I'm not at liberty to discuss it, sir. Please, sir."

He looked from one inscrutable face to the next, and he realized that they weren't kidding. As if on cue, Miral began to squall in the back room.

"As you can hear, gentlemen, I've got a little one to take care of. I'm not about to—"

"Understood, sir. We'll take the child with us. She'll be well looked after while you are undergoing questioning."

"No. Oh, no. I'm not about to hand my little girl over to some stranger from Starfleet Security." Even as he spoke, he hurried to the nursery and picked up his crying daughter.

"I'm afraid you don't have a choice." The three men had followed him into the nursery, where their formal stance and gray, mustard, and black uniforms were sharply at odds with the twirling mobile and soft pastel hues of the walls and ceiling. Their commanding officer moved his hand, ever so slightly, to the phaser on his hip. Tom didn't miss the gesture.

He held Miral closer to him. "At least let me contact someone I know to take care of her while I'm gone," he said, almost pleading. The leader seemed to consider it but didn't answer right away.

"Oh, come on!" Tom said, exasperated and starting to get just a little bit frightened.

"Very well."

Paris went to the computer. "Computer, contact Admiral Owen Paris. Message is urgent."

It seemed to take forever for his father's face to appear. The elder Paris looked groggy, but he brightened at the sight of his son and granddaughter.

"Hi, Dad. Sorry to wake you at this hour."

"Is everything all right?"

Tom glanced over at the emotionless face of the head of the little party that had shown up on his doorstep. "That remains to be seen," he said. "Seems that I'm wanted for questioning about something and it apparently can't wait until a decent hour."

Admiral Paris looked grave, but not surprised. He nodded and sighed. "I was hoping you'd be kept out of it," he said, "but I suppose they need to talk to everyone."

"You know what this is all about?" Tom asked, startled.

"Not entirely, but I have an inkling. You'll need to go with them, Tom."

"Well, yeah, but I've got a cute little problem with going with them right now," he said. "Can you—will you and Mom look after her?" His voice faltered. "I don't know when I'll be back."

"Of course, son. You won't be gone long."

"Thank you, Dad." Tom looked down at his daughter, felt his throat tighten, and hoped his father was right.

The ritual baths, chanting, meditation, and preparation were finally over. Torres was about to depart, finally, for the Challenge of Spirit. She knew she had a few minutes of privacy left before Logt was to come and get her, so she quickly unfolded the note her mother had left her and read it one last time, trying to memorize it:

> My dearest 'Lanna,
>
> As I write this, they are waiting outside for me. They think I am embarking on the Challenge of Spirit in the usual manner, and that, if I survive the proper length of time, I will return. If I do not return, I will be assumed dead. Perhaps I may be, but I think not.
>
> I am waiting for you. A few days ago I had a vision that was so powerfully vivid that I know that on some level, it was real. I was on the Barge of the Dead, and you came to lift my dishonor. In this vision, you took the first step toward making peace with the two parts of you that have always been at war. I believe that you were there, with me, in some way. Whether or not this is so, I hope to learn directly from your own lips.
>
> I am taking the Challenge, but I will be at the place I have indicated on this map.
>
> You found me in a dream once before. You will find me again. We have much to speak of. I will see you again, dearest 'Lanna.
>
> Find me.

"I will, Mother," said Torres aloud. She went over the map one final time, then held the piece of paper to the lamp flame. An orange tongue of fire licked the paper, blackening it. Torres dropped it into a small bowl and watched it burn, curling in on itself until it was nothing but ashes.

She was so lost in thought watching the twisting paper that the loud knock on the door made her jump. Torres rose and composed herself as Logt entered. The older woman looked her up and down, eyeing the ritual garb B'Elanna had sewn herself. Part of the required preparation, sewing it had taken hours, and was spotted with magenta blood here and there, but she had completed the task and was rather proud of the end result.

"I suppose you'll do," Logt said.

"I'm not appearing on a stage," Torres snapped.

"No. You're appearing before Kahless, and that is much more important. You were granted special dispensation to even undertake the Challenge, B'Elanna Torres, half human as you are. It can be revoked at any time if you prove yourself unworthy. And that would be dishonor indeed. Come."

Torres followed Logt as she led her down a stone stairway barely big enough for a single person to pass. Instead of the temperature dropping, as would have been normal for a descent into the ground, Torres noticed that it was growing hotter.

The lava caves. Of course, this would be where the final rite would be. These were Klingons, after all. One wouldn't just say, "Okay, I'm off to the Challenge of Spirit. See you when I get back." She smiled a little to herself; she was starting to think like Tom.

The heat grew more intense. Torres began to sweat profusely and it grew difficult to breathe. She tried hard not to pant but heard Logt's chuckle.

"I knew you were too soft for this," the warrior said. "Miral was made of sterner stuff."

"You're going to eat those words when I return with—" B'Elanna had almost said "when I return with my mother." She amended quickly, "With honor."

Logt paused, turned, and gave B'Elanna a thoroughly appraising look. "Something is not right about this," she said. "I feel . . ."

"What?" B'Elanna challenged, worried that somehow Logt would guess her deception, but Logt did not answer. She scrutinized B'Elanna for a moment longer, then shrugged, something that wasn't easy to do with all that leather armor.

"It is of no matter," Logt said. "If you return, all honor debts are paid. If you don't, then you've gotten what you deserve for your arrogance."

They continued the descent in silence. B'Elanna wondered if the hot air was scorching her lungs. She started to grow faint, and willed herself to stay conscious with all the ferocity that she knew was in her. She had been kept ignorant of the intricacies of the ritual; all she knew was that it would represent a severing of who she had been prior to this moment. When B'Elanna Torres returned from her Challenge of Spirit, she would no longer be the same woman who departed for it.

If she returned.

Angrily she told herself to stop it. She could not even entertain the thought of failure. Her mother was out there somewhere, dead or alive, and B'Elanna was going to find her.

The stairway widened to a small room as it ended. Logt stepped away from B'Elanna and suddenly brandished a knife. Before Torres could react, Logt was upon her, but B'Elanna felt no pain. Her clothing suddenly hung loosely upon her and she clutched it to her. Logt had cut B'Elanna's gown, not her body. *It took forever for me to make this!* Torres thought. She was somehow more distressed that all her hard work had been to produce a garment that would get cut to pieces within seconds of the ritual's start than she would have been if her body had been targeted.

A door was flung open and waves of heat rolled out. Logt shoved and B'Elanna stumbled forward, still clutching the last shreds of clothing and dignity.

Three Klingon women stood before her, as naked as she would be had she not literally held her clothes to her body. They were not, however, in the least bit vulnerable in their nudity. Rather, they were intimidating. One of them threw back her head and screamed a wordless cry. The other two dove forward and snatched the strips that were all that remained of B'Elanna's gown and tossed them into the bubbling pit of lava in the center of the room.

Automatically B'Elanna covered herself, but the two women who had stripped her now clutched her hands and pulled them down to her sides.

"You are to be reborn, B'Elanna Torres," the woman who was clearly the highest-ranking priestess said, walking to her slowly, proudly. In her hands, she held a pot of some vile-smelling ointment.

"You will go naked into the world, as you came

naked into it. You entered the world covered only with
the blood and fluids from your mother's womb. Fire
births you here."

She stepped forward and smeared B'Elanna's face,
hair, and body with the putrid goop. B'Elanna recognized the smell of blood among other scents that made
her want to vomit. The heat and the stench were getting
to her and the room began to spin. She held on to consciousness with grim determination. Now the woman
was smearing soot all over her.

Her mind flashed back to her years as a child in the
monastery. She'd never encountered anything like this.
The rituals she'd participated in were flamboyant and
showy, with lots of talk and pretty costumes. This was
in dark, deadly earnest.

They threw her hard to the ground. B'Elanna grunted
as her body slammed into the warm stone. Something
was smeared over her hands.

"Now bathe your hands in the blood of the earth, in
the fire that consumes and destroys."

She stared up at the priestess in horror. The lava was
nothing less than rock so hot it was liquid. To immerse
her hands in it would be to char them right off. The
priestess smirked.

"The mongrel hesitates."

The derogatory term spurred B'Elanna on. Some part
of her reasoned that they would not ask it of her unless
she had some chance of succeeding. And if she burned
her hands off, well, the Doctor would no doubt come
up with something suitable to replace them.

She was too woozy to rise, so she crawled along the

stone floor to the pit. The heat blasting off it was almost unbearable. *For you, Mother.*

Uttering a cry, she shoved her hands into the lava.

And felt nothing.

Part of her screamed that it was a miracle, that she had passed the test. The other part of her calmly reasoned that whatever they had smeared on her hands was protecting her from the heat. Idly, she wondered what the stuff was.

But then strong hands were grabbing her and pulling her back from the pit, even as she realized that if she had lingered much longer, her face would have begun to blister.

Dazed, sick, every muscle quivering, she did not protest as they hauled her to her feet. The priestess held her face firmly between her strong hands. B'Elanna stared up into her fierce, sharp-toothed, painted face, and found her beautiful.

"You have been accepted. You may undertake the Challenge. Go forth, and wrest honor from the wilderness."

B'Elanna was spun around and almost fell. There came a loud boom as a door was opened in front of her. Cool air rushed in and she gulped it deeply. So engrossed was she in simply breathing in the pure night air, so sweet after the sickly toxins of the lava, that it took a moment for the priestess's words to register.

She was about to step into Boreth's notorious wilderness clad only in blood and ashes, with no food, no water, and no weapons.

B'Elanna Torres almost broke.

Then she summoned courage she never knew she possessed, and forced her head up. She straightened to her full height, and heard murmurs of approval behind her. Unsteadily, deliberately, B'Elanna Torres moved first one foot, then the other, walking into the unknown with her head held high.

Chapter
18

LIBBY WAS FURIOUS.

Harry had been supposed to meet her outside of the Green Dragon well over an hour ago. It was one of the few restaurants still in business since the fiasco of the HoloStrike, as the wags were calling it, and she'd had to pull some strings to even get reservations.

She stood outside in the driving rain because she wouldn't be able to see him coming if she waited inside, and she wanted a piece of him. Badly. She'd never been stood up before in her life and wasn't taking it well at all.

Li Wu, a flesh-and-blood waiter and therefore as rare in San Francisco as a flying horse, cautiously stuck his head out.

"Miss Webber?" he called, looking apologetic. "Boss

says he's going to have to open up your reservation in five minutes if Harry doesn't come."

Shivering, she turned and glared at him. Wu shrank back from her anger and she tried to compose herself, shoving back her sopping hair with one hand.

"Sorry, Li. It was awfully nice of Mr. Wang to hold it for me so long. Tell him that won't be necessary. I don't think Harry's coming, so I'm just going to head on home."

He looked embarrassed and sorry for her, but merely nodded. "Maybe sometime next month," he offered.

Libby grimaced. It would take about that long to get a reservation, if the HoloStrike didn't end soon. The Green Dragon had always employed humans as waiters, busboys, and cooks, a tradition that had always made it quaint and endearing in Chinatown and now made it one of the most popular places in the city. Wang's vision, a gamble when he had started, had certainly paid off.

"Maybe," she said.

"Wait!" exclaimed Li. He ducked back outside and reappeared a few moments later with a small, enclosed cup. "Got some egg drop soup for you to sip on the way home. Your favorite."

Libby almost cried. She would have hugged Li had she not been soaking wet. Instead she gave him a big, runny-makeup smile, and waved good-bye.

Of course, she had to walk. In the rain. Finding a public transporter that actually had a human to operate it was difficult, and because of safety reasons, any that didn't have an operator had been shut down. On a balmy night it was a pleasant walk despite the hilliness of San Francisco's terrain, but tonight Libby soaked her nicest pair of shoes splashing angrily through puddles. She paused occasionally to take cautious sips of the hot soup, which warmed her enough to continue.

At one point she turned a corner too fast and twisted her ankle on the rain-slicked pavement. The half-finished carton of egg drop soup went flying. She went down in an ungracious heap and landed hard on her knees. When she tried to rise, her foot behaved strangely, and for a dreadful second she thought she'd broken her leg and was not feeling anything due to shock. It took her a moment and a few steps to realize she'd merely snapped the heel off her shoe.

She wanted to shriek, but instead took a deep breath, removed both shoes, and walked to the transporter site in stocking feet.

Libby was shaking violently by the time she materialized in her small cabin in Maine. Rowena rubbed up against her and then stalked off, insulted by Libby's soaking-wet leg. Indigo didn't even bother. Libby stumbled over to the computer, expecting to see at least an apologetic message from Harry, but there was nothing. She muttered dark curses against Harry's name and shed clothing on the way to the sonic shower.

Finally, wrapped in a thick robe, she replicated a mug of hot cocoa and took a few warm, soothing sips. She was hungry, but that could wait. She tried to contact Harry, but there was no response. She left a very curt message and leaned back in her chair.

For the first time, it occurred to her that something

might be wrong. She'd simply assumed Harry had gotten engrossed in something and lost track of the time, but she hadn't seen his sheepish face on the screen when she tried to contact him.

She put a call through to the Green Dragon. Wang's face appeared and he looked as if he were treading on eggshells.

"Hi, Mr. Wang. Harry didn't show up there by any chance?"

Wang shook his graying head. "No, Miss Webber. No sign of him. You know I'd have let him contact you if he had been here."

"Yes, of course you would, I should have thought of that. Well, if he does show, I'll want to talk to him."

Wang grinned. "I'm sure you will."

Next, Libby tried Harry's parents. Maybe one of them had taken ill. Harry was nothing if not a good son. As was their wont, both the Kims' faces appeared. They always did things together.

"Libby, dear! What a surprise!" said Mrs. Kim.

"It is so good to see you!" enthused Mr. Kim, as if she and Harry hadn't had dinner with them four nights ago.

"Good evening, Mr. and Mrs. Kim. I'm so sorry to be bothering you so late, but I was wondering, is Harry with you?"

Immediately she knew she'd said the wrong thing. Their lined faces filled with concern.

"No, dear, we thought he was with you. Going out to the Green Dragon. It was so sweet of you to get reservations in the midst of this dreadful strike, I can't imagine that Harry would forget," said Mr. Kim.

"Something's wrong," said Mrs. Kim with conviction. "Something terrible has happened. I know it."

Anxious to calm them, Libby smacked her forehead with the heel of her hand and laughed. "Silly me! Tonight was when he was playing poker with his friends from *Voyager*," she lied. *"Tomorrow* is when we were supposed to go to the Green Dragon. I can't believe I got the dates confused." She smiled radiantly. "I guess I was just so looking forward to dinner at the restaurant that I wanted it to be a day sooner than it was."

Mr. Kim smiled indulgently. "Young people are just too eager," he chastised gently. "Good things are worth waiting for, not rushing."

"Harry plays poker?" said Mrs. Kim, frowning. "I'm not at all sure I approve of him gambling."

Libby realized that she'd just gotten Harry into some hot water, but better that than panicking his parents.

"Well, it's late," she said, faking a yawn. "Sorry to have disturbed you."

"Never a bother, my dear," said Mr. Kim sweetly.

"You tell Harry that I'm going to talk to him about this bad habit of his," Harry's mother warned.

"I will. Good night." She smiled broadly. The grin ebbed the minute their faces disappeared from the viewscreen.

Harry hadn't shown up at the restaurant. He wasn't home and his parents thought he was with her.

Although Mrs. Kim worried too much about her son, Libby was beginning to think she was right. Something had happened to Harry. And she was going to find out what.

Director Covington seemed surprised and more than a trifle annoyed to receive Libby's message.

"I'm two minutes away from a very important meeting, Agent Webber. Can this wait?"

"No," said Libby firmly, startling them both with her determination. "Harry's gone missing. I can't contact him anywhere."

Covington smiled slightly. "Sometimes men don't want to be found by their girlfriends," she said, gently.

Libby shook her dark head, and her curls bobbed vigorously with the movement.

"Not Harry. He's not like that. I also tried to contact his friends, people like Tom Paris and Lyssa Campbell. No one knows where any of them is. I was wondering if something was going on."

"Oh," said Covington. Then, as her pale gold brows drew together, *"Oh.* Agent Webber, I want you to be able to view this meeting." Her long fingers flew. "Admiral Montgomery is coming here in just a few moments, and I think you'd better be present, as it were. My little fly on the wall."

"Do you think— Oh my God, Montgomery isn't kidnapping people? Why? What does Harry have to do with *Voyager*'s technology? Do you think he and the others stumbled onto Montgomery's negotiations with the Orions? Does this have anything to do with—"

Covington's head came up and her pale eyes were fierce. For the first time, Libby saw the steel behind a woman who had to be strong in order to be where she was. Covington had always struck her as friendly, but now Libby saw that she could be harsh when she needed to be.

"Agent Webber!" The words cracked like a whip, and Libby had to consciously refrain from flinching. "These wild suppositions will avail us nothing. I expect you to behave as befits your station."

Libby knew she was right. "Yes, ma'am," she said. She was starting to get hysterical, and that wouldn't help anyone.

Covington softened. "I need you at the top of your game now more than ever, Libby," she said, using her subordinate's first name, something she rarely did. "Can I count on you?"

Libby nodded. "You can," she said.

"Good." Covington punched a few more buttons and Libby's view of the scene pulled back so that she could see more of the room. There came a soft chime. "That's him," said Covington. "Watch him closely and we'll discuss the conversation when it's over. I won't be able to see or hear you, but you can see and hear us. And of course, everything you witness here must be held in the strictest confidence. Understood?"

"Yes, ma'am," said Libby. She swallowed hard, tried to calm her racing heart, and leaned forward.

Libby had always respected Admiral Kenneth Montgomery, although he was a distant and chilly man, hard to truly like. He'd been a solid rock during the Dominion War, one of the real heroes to emerge from the conflict. But now, knowing what she did, Libby couldn't even give him the credit for what he'd done. He was a traitor, and worse, he might be responsible for hurting Harry. She looked at his broad shoulders and saw not strength, but brute force; at his brown, lined face and saw not the care of a compassionate man for countless lives, but only the marks of frowns and scowls.

He strode into Covington's office as if he owned it, glancing about and grimacing in distaste.

"It's a bit of a cliché for a Covert Operations director to keep her guests so in the dark, isn't it?" he said without preamble. He did not reach out to shake her hand, and she didn't rise.

"You light your office your way, I'll light mine my way," she said.

"You should get out more, Brenna. You're getting pale sitting alone in the dark."

Covington smiled icily, dislike plain in her eyes. "I'll tell you what. You don't talk about what the sun hasn't done to my face, and I won't talk about what it *has* done to yours."

Libby snorted, even though she knew it was meanspirited. Montgomery's brown face was indeed more lined than it ought to be.

"Enough pleasantries," Covington said. "What brings you here, Admiral? Thought you'd have your hands full with taking *Voyager* apart piece by technological piece." She waved her hand absently in the direction of a chair and he took it.

"Wish I had time to do that," he said, "but I seem to have my hands full with other problems. I was first saddled with the holographic strike, and now I've got this damn Borg outbreak to try to keep quiet."

Libby gasped, her hand flying to her throat. She was grateful the conversation only went one way. Borg? Here on Earth? What was going on? To her astonishment, Covington didn't bat an eye. Either she was one cool customer or else she had already known about it.

"I'm not sure I understand—what does either of these things have to do with *Voyager?* Or have you been pulled off that project?"

"No, I'm still on the project." Montgomery's voice showed his irritation. "Didn't you read the report I sent out?"

Covington smiled with false sweetness. "Quite a lot of reports cross my desk, Admiral. One such was the one written by one of my agents who brought the Borg virus to your attention in the first place and advised the Xakarian flu cover-up strategy you're taking now. I perused your report but I didn't have time to read it in depth."

Montgomery sighed. "All right, let me recap for you. We're pretty sure the Doctor was involved in rabble-rousing the holograms to strike, and we also think that the appearance of Borg around the globe has to do with *Voyager's* return."

Again, the Borg, here on Earth. Libby couldn't believe what she was hearing. The Xakarian flu outbreak was merely a cover-up to hide a—a Borg virus? It seemed impossible. This couldn't be—and yet she had no reason to doubt Montgomery or Covington.

Regarding the Doctor, though, she had no trouble knowing what to think. She'd met the Doctor. He was acerbic, true, and a bit full of himself, but he was also charming and compassionate. He wouldn't do such a thing.

Or would he? No one had been harmed. He cared passionately about holographic rights . . . could the witty EMH really be behind the strike? And how could *Voyager* be involved with Borg suddenly appearing on Earth? It was all almost too much to comprehend.

They had continued speaking, and she realized she had been so busy digesting the information that she'd missed a large part of the conversation. What kind of a spy was she? Angrily, she calmed herself and strained to hear.

". . . contain the scope," Montgomery was saying.

"Naturally," agreed Covington. "The panic that would ensue could possibly cause more damage than the virus itself."

"I'm here for the SOP check-in with all department heads. Any covert operations taking place at any of these sites?" He handed her a padd.

Libby wished he'd just name the places, but trusted that if she needed to know anything Covington would tell her.

Covington held on to the padd for a moment before looking at it. "Believe me, if any of my agents spotted your well-meaning security guards mucking about, we'd know it before you did." She scanned the list, then shook her fair head. "I don't think so. If you'll tell me your plans and what you know so far, I'll tell you if I have anything that would conflict."

Montgomery didn't seem to like it, but obviously he

had no choice. Libby knew what damage could result if a covert operation was accidentally uncovered by well-meaning friendly troops. Years of work could be lost, a criminal could go free, and worse, people could die if their deep covers were exposed.

"Long-range sensors haven't detected any Borg ships in the area. The threat isn't from a cube; it's from something right here on Earth. It's not assimilation in the sense that we're familiar with the term—no drones beaming down and sticking their tubes into people, then hauling them off and severing limbs and replacing eyes."

Libby shuddered. She'd never met a Borg, thank God, but Harry had told her the stories, and that was enough for her to sense how utterly terrifying the creatures were.

"It appears to be a virus of some sort, and as with most viruses, it targets those who have the least well developed immune systems. Children, old people, the ill. Thus far, anyway."

"What do you mean by that?"

"There's every evidence that it's only a matter of time before healthy adults who have contracted this—this disease will succumb. It's taking longer because their immune systems can fight off what the body sees as an infection, but I fear these twenty-three cases are just the first small wave."

"Twenty-three?" Covington seemed startled. "I had no idea it was that many. I'd heard reports of only about seven."

Montgomery glowered. "We had seven confirmed outbreaks at the time I sent out the report. Now that we know what to look for, we've been able to isolate and quarantine twenty-three cases and their immediate families in various places across the globe. Which is where you come in."

Covington arched an eyebrow.

"All of this started when *Voyager* docked here on Earth. Not a minute before and only a month afterward. That ship is crammed to the gills with technology we don't understand, including several Borg modifications." Montgomery made a face. "To think that that Janeway woman collaborated with the Borg . . . it's enough to make your stomach turn. Especially now that they're responsible for bringing the Borg to Earth. We'd kept the planet safe, until now."

"Do you have direct evidence that this was caused by *Voyager?*"

"I've got enough to go on. We can track one infected child directly to Janeway. Besides, what else could it possibly be? Too bad the Borg Entreaty got shot down. We could use it now. I've got thirty people working on creating cover stories alone. The Xakarian flu story is still holding water, but it won't for much longer."

"Yes," drawled Covington. "That pesky free press."

"You can't tell me the head of Sector 001 Covert Ops wouldn't be glad of the Borg Entreaty along about now."

"From what I hear, you don't need the Borg Entreaty to haul people in and keep them imprisoned without charges."

"Damn right. We're at war with the Borg, and Starfleet deems these people enemy combatants until we know for sure they're not."

Libby knew her mouth was hanging open in astonishment. Everyone knew about the failed Borg Entreaty of 2367. It had been one of the most passionate, heart-breaking speeches ever given in Federation history, hard on the heels of the Borg attack on Wolf 359. There had been a wave of panic and fear that had swept through the Federation following that disastrous incident, and when the widow of a Starfleet junior officer who had been killed there had spoken from her full and breaking heart, everyone had been inclined to sympathize.

Julie Elliot and her husband had been young, just recently married, and Julie had learned two days before her husband's death that she was pregnant.

Her heartfelt plea, known as the Borg Entreaty, had been eloquent and poignant. At the core of it, it begged to enact a waiver of the rights due Federation citizens if any Borg involvement or influence was suspected. Anyone could be arrested and detained for the course of a full year without specific charges being filed if sufficient evidence could be provided that the individual was being manipulated by the Borg. It was odd, to have such a lyrical, famous speech plead not for freedoms, but for imprisonment and a waiving of inherent rights.

While Elliot's tearful words had fallen on sympathetic ears, and the Borg were dreadful and terrifying, the motion had not passed. It was too much, even for that emotional time.

So this was what had happened to Harry, to Tom and to Lyssa and the other hundred and fifty or so people who had served loyally for seven years on *Voyager.* Her lover and friends had been hauled off to prison, just because this pompous Starfleet—

"And of course, we're going to need your agents to find out who they had contact with."

"What?" cried Covington, starting up in her chair.

"You heard me. I need Covert Ops to start tracking down everyone every *Voyager* crew member had contact with from the minute they beamed on Earth."

Libby had never seen Covington at a loss for words before. "You mean to tell me," she said slowly, "that you want my agents assigned to finding out every single person that every single *Voyager* crew member made love to, had dinner with, met, shook hands with, or passed on the street over the last six weeks?"

"That's exactly what I'm telling you."

"You're insane. That's impossible. I haven't the staff to spare. I'd have to call about half of them out of deep cover and remove them from operations that have been in place for years. Have your staff do the grunt work if you want it done so badly."

Montgomery smiled, then handed her a padd. "These are your orders from the president," he said. "You are to comply with everything I've asked of you. This is a Federation-wide threat, not a Starfleet internal problem. You find the civilians. My people will handle the Starfleet personnel."

Judging by Covington's expression as she perused the padd, the order was genuine.

"And by the way, you commandeered Trevor Blake some time ago. I want him back."

Covington seemed to be having difficulty controlling her emotions. "Blake has been assigned to Covert Operations. He's not completed his mission with me yet."

"Didn't you hear what I said? You are to comply—"

"You're in my realm now, Montgomery," snarled Covington, looking like a tiger. "You want Blake? You get the president to order him off his assignment. You don't get to do it. Blake's needed here."

"What the hell is a scientist needed for Covert Operations for over four years?" Montgomery exploded. "I need him on my team! Tell me why you need him so badly and maybe I'll reconsider."

Covington stiffened, her slim body as rigid as if it were made of metal.

"That's classified information, on a need-to-know basis. And you, my old friend, don't need to know."

"Why all this secrecy? Why are you hiding this from me?"

She smiled, nastily. "That's why it's called *Covert* Operations, you—" With a huge effort, she got herself under control. For a long moment, they stood glaring at each other. Finally, Montgomery straightened to his full height.

"Start with the command crew first—Janeway, Chakotay, and so on." He rose. "I look forward to reading your report as soon as you know anything."

It was a dismissal, and both Libby and Covington knew it. Libby's cheeks burned with embarrassment for her boss, but Covington's pale face didn't change color.

"If you're trying to keep this quiet," she said, "this is a pretty poor way to go about it."

"We're playing up the HoloStrike," said Montgomery. "That's enough to keep people's attention focused. And I trust you and your agents to be discreet in your assignments. Also, tell your people to be watchful for the symptoms. The Borg virus isn't immediate; it can take a while before it manifests completely. They should watch for fever, lack of energy, and loss of appetite."

Libby thought that the symptoms were vague enough to describe a few dozen harmless conditions and wondered how many people dealing with a simple bug were now going to be imprisoned for the bad luck of getting sick.

"Good-bye, Brenna." He left.

Covington watched him go, her eyes boring holes in his back. Libby heard the hiss of the door closing. Covington took a deep breath and touched the controls on her desk.

"Did you get all that, Agent Webber?" she asked.

Libby had to clear her throat before she could speak. "Yes, ma'am. Indeed I did."

"It answers the question of what happened to Mr. Kim. And it certainly temporarily removes many people who could stand in the way of someone trying to deliver *Voyager*'s technology to the Orion Syndicate. Hell, for all we know, the Syndicate could even be behind the virus."

"Montgomery is growing increasingly powerful," said Libby quietly. "There aren't many who *can* stand in his way right now. All he has to do is point a finger and suddenly they're in prison."

"It's an alarming thought," agreed Covington.

"Ma'am . . . are you really going to take your agents off deep-cover assignments?"

"I'll do what I have to do, Agent Webber, as will you."

Libby nodded. "Shall I turn myself in, then?"

Covington considered. "No, not just yet. I know where I can find you. I want you to stick to Montgomery. Watch him. Of course, I can't ask you to hinder the investigation."

"Of course not," Libby said dutifully. But the implication was there. "Do you—how long do you think they'll hold the *Voyager* crew?"

"I don't know. I'm guessing not long, especially if they want to keep this hush-hush. It's probably just a matter of asking them questions and running tests. But we'll have to see."

Libby returned to perusing old reports with a renewed vigor. She now had a personal grudge against Admiral Kenneth Montgomery, the traitorous mole who had imprisoned her beloved, and she was going to see that the bastard was brought down.

Chapter

19

IT HAD BEEN A LONG NIGHT, but Li Wu was only moderately tired. A night of brisk business always energized him. The rain had cleared up shortly after Libby Webber had given up on her date—Li would never stand her up if he were dating her—and the Green Dragon hummed with activity well into the small hours of the morning.

Wang had gone home around eleven-thirty, after bidding the last guests good night. Li Wu had stayed to make sure the kitchen was properly cleaned up, the dining area spotless in anticipation of the crowds that would start showing up tomorrow for lunch, and that in general all was in order. He had closed up the shop and was about a quarter of the way home when it started raining again.

He swore. He'd left his umbrella in the ceramic, dragon-shaped stand by the door. Stupid San Francisco weather. Sighing, Li turned up his collar against the cold splash of the raindrops and half-ran back to the restaurant.

He had just opened the door and was reaching for the umbrella when the Green Dragon exploded.

When Janeway entered the prison's sickbay, she was prepared for anything, except what she got.

She and her entire crew had been treated with suspicion and thinly veiled hostility. Only the command crew had been informed as to why they were arrested and brought in, and they had been ordered to secrecy. She was pleased that Montgomery seemed a bit embarrassed, but not mollified in the slightest. In fact, she was outraged. If any crew in Starfleet had reason to hate the Borg and to want to keep them away from Earth, it was *Voyager*'s. They were being treated like common criminals, summarily hauled in and grilled. It was the opposite of what should have been done. There were three people in prison who knew the Borg better than anyone, and one of those had more medical knowledge than any other ten doctors combined.

There were too many things she didn't know, either, and that angered her as well. She knew that somehow, Kevin Johnson had been turned into a partial Borg, and that he and his family had disappeared. Where, she didn't know. Allegedly they and Molly were under quarantine, but she wasn't sure if she believed that.

She didn't know if Kevin was the only one, or if Borg were spontaneously popping out of every gopher hole from San Francisco to China. She didn't know why Seven and Icheb were suspected or if they would ever be released.

So when she walked into sickbay, it was with her head held high, her eyes narrowed in defiance, and a chip on her shoulder the size of a small shuttlecraft.

The doctor had his back to her when she and her "escort" entered. "I'll be with you in just a moment," he said, holding up his left index finger and finishing entering data with his other hand. He turned around and his eyes lit up as he recognized her.

"Admiral Janeway! I've so wanted to meet you." The light in his bright eyes faded somewhat. "Although not under these circumstances. Thank you, Lieutenant, that will do."

The burly guard left, and the admiral and the doctor stood regarding one another. Janeway had to admit he was strikingly handsome, with his thick, curly dark hair and intense blue eyes. A strong, masculine face with a sensitive mouth was framed by small dots disappearing into his collar. A Trill, then. He extended a hand and indicated the biobed.

"Please, Admiral. I don't like this any better than you do. I'm sure I won't find anything to report, so let's get this over with quickly."

"Oh, why the rush?" said Janeway acidly. "I'm in no real hurry to get back to my cell."

"If I don't find anything, Admiral," said the doctor, "then you'll be released."

Janeway raised an eyebrow, trying not to hope too hard. "In that case . . . ." She hopped up onto the biobed.

"Thank you." He picked up a medical tricorder. "My

name is Jarem Kaz. I'm very sorry for what you and your crew has had to go through, but it really was necessary."

"Was it?" she challenged him. He didn't meet her eyes. "The command staff was informed that the Borg are somehow involved," she continued, watching him closely for his reaction. "I don't suppose you'd care to fill me in on any further details about what's been going on."

Kaz smiled, ruefully, Janeway thought. "I wish I could, believe me. What's happening here is frightening on a variety of levels."

"You speak pretty freely for a top-level security clearance doctor," Janeway said.

Again, Kaz smiled, his eyes on the instrument. "One of my former hosts was the equivalent of a Poet Laureate on Trill, and the one after that was a Maquis. It's a combination that leads to lots of lyrical free thinking."

Their eyes met, and Janeway liked what she saw in their blue depths. She returned his smile.

"I gather that all those you've previously examined have been permitted to be released? Or did you find a few Borg in my crew?"

"Besides Seven of Nine and Icheb, you mean?"

Janeway stiffened. "They have been liberated from the collective. I'd bet my life that they are not being manipulated by the Borg in any way."

"And I agree with you a hundred percent," said Kaz, surprising her. "I've said as much to Admiral Montgomery, but my opinion doesn't seem to be enough to bring about their release, or even get them a regeneration chamber."

Janeway decided to take the risk. "You said you were a free thinker, Doctor. Are you enough of one to do what's right?" she challenged.

"Admiral, you know I have my orders."

"If they involve holding people you know to be innocent who could help you stop a Borg infestation, then they're stupid orders," she said, bluntly.

"I'm not privy to everything. There could be logical reasons why Starfleet is proceeding in this manner."

"Do you really think so?"

His blue eyes told her all she needed to know. The seed of doubt had been planted.

Kaz sighed and stepped back. "Your blood pressure and your heart rate are slightly elevated—no surprise there, considering the circumstances. Your cholesterol has dropped slightly from its baseline. Apparently prison agrees with you."

"I don't agree with it," said Janeway. "As a matter of fact I'm—"

The door hissed open. A guard rushed in. "You need to see this. Both of you."

He touched the screen of Kaz's computer, and an image of Oliver Baines appeared. He was in the middle of a speech.

". . . I deeply regret," he was saying. "But there are always victims in a war, even the most just war. Holograms are not like those who made them. We—they—obtain no pleasure in murder. All of the attacks last night were on buildings that we believed to be empty. If the Federation had responded by calling a council to discuss holographic rights when the HoloStrike first began, as we requested a full three weeks ago, there would have been no need to escalate to violence. We grieve the loss of life, but it will not slow us down. A deleted hologram has the right to be mourned as much as a slain organic. Until we have equality, we will not rest." He smiled, as if at a joke. "We don't need to."

His image disappeared. Janeway whirled on the guard. "He said something about loss of life. What's happened?"

The guard didn't reply at first, looking uncertainly at Kaz. Kaz uttered an expletive and said, "I've given her a clean bill of health, she's about to walk out of here a free woman. Talk to us!"

"Yes, sir," said the guard. "There was a coordinated attack on hundreds of buildings across the world last night. The HoloRevolutionaries under Oliver Baines have claimed full responsibility for it. Eight people were killed. They say that they assumed that the buildings were empty at the time. They were restaurants, theaters, sports arenas—places that used to have holograms but now have living people providing the entertainment. Apparently the attack was not supposed to have resulted in casualties."

"Intention is all well and good, but when there are dead bodies it goes out the window," Janeway said, pressing her lips together. "Dammit. Baines should have listened to the Doctor. He's now a murderer, intentionally or not. Starfleet might have ignored a strike, but they're not going to ignore corpses."

Kaz looked troubled. "I agree with you, Admiral."

He turned and regarded her intently. "And I fear for your Doctor."

So did Janeway.

Libby was surviving on strong coffee and catnaps.

In the time since the conversation between Covington and Montgomery had taken place, she had downloaded every scrap of information she had access to. It was a lot. Grim determination buoyed her at first and kept sleep at bay, but as the hours stretched into days, she found herself surrendering to twenty-minute naps to keep from lapsing into deeper, more time-consuming sleep. She'd need stimulants if she had to keep this up much longer.

She had reread Covington's report on Montgomery, going over it with the figurative fine-toothed comb, and found in it more than enough circumstantial evidence to damn Montgomery to a lifetime in prison for treason. But the odd thing was, when she tried to cross-reference the information using other documentation, almost everything fell apart. A few hours ago, she'd summoned all her computer training and successfully accessed the less-secure levels of Montgomery's own office. Nothing there helped her case against him, either.

Even worse, the deeper she dug, the more she found discrepancies. Covington's report had Montgomery in one place, supposedly meeting with his Orion Syndicate contact, when Libby knew for a fact that he'd been elsewhere. Still other things were supposed intra-office memos that Libby found no record of in Montgomery's own computer systems. What was going on?

She leaned back and rubbed her gritty, red eyes. Maybe she should take a break, have a good, long sleep and a solid meal. She knew from experience that sometimes working too hard made one careless, likely to overlook something that was right under one's nose. But time was passing too quickly. Montgomery was now in charge of several projects, all so conveniently interlinked, and if he were allowed to get away with it—

Her console chimed softly. Someone was trying to reach her. Covington again, no doubt. Maybe she had more information.

Wearily Libby touched the controls, and her eyes widened to see the face of Harry Kim.

"Harry!" she cried. She almost said, *They let you go!* But just in time said instead, "Where have you been?"

He smiled, looking as tired as she knew she must appear to him. "I'm not permitted to say, but I'm back now. I'm sorry I stood you up. If I'd been able to contact you, I would have."

"I know, honey," she said. "Whatever it is, I'm sure you had a good reason."

He looked solemn. "Did you hear about Li?"

She bit her lip. She wasn't given to hysterics, but she'd had so little sleep recently and the thought of poor Li— "Yes, I did. It's horrible."

They fell silent. Then Harry blurted, "I want to see you."

Libby had a brief, violent war with herself. There was so much more to read, so many pieces of a puzzle to put together. And yet, she was so tired that she knew she wasn't thinking clearly.

"I'll be right there," she said softly.

"Any news?" Irene Hansen's face, normally so bright and cheerful, looked aged and gray. Janeway felt for her.

"I'm sorry. They're not going to release her or Icheb any time soon, but they're being well treated." It was a partial truth. Seven and Icheb's unique part-Borg nature required unique treatment, which they weren't receiving. Thank God Dr. Kaz was a sympathetic man.

"Will they let me see her yet?"

Janeway shook her head. "I'm afraid not, Ms. Hansen. How are you holding up?"

Irene sighed deeply. "Well enough, I suppose. The house is so empty without her, Admiral."

"Please, call me Kathryn."

"Then I'm Irene, dear."

"Irene," said Janeway, "I'm going to send Lieutenant Commander Tuvok to your house. We're going to transport you somewhere a little less well known."

"No," said Irene, her firmness surprising Janeway. "This is my home. I'm not moving. Seven needs a safe place to come home to."

Janeway chose her words carefully. She was, of course, forbidden to reveal what she knew of the encroaching Borg virus. But if things continued as they had, soon the world would know. And if the public knew, then prison would be the safest place on Earth for Seven and Icheb.

"I have some information that leads me to believe

you might be safer elsewhere for a little while," Janeway said at last. "I ask you to trust me on this."

Irene Hansen lifted her head and narrowed her eyes in an expression so familiar that Janeway almost laughed. How often had she seen Seven do exactly this?

"I appreciate your concern, Kathryn. But I'm fine where I am."

Janeway inclined her head, acknowledging defeat. "If you feel threatened by anything, at any time—"

"Then I'll know who to contact," Irene finished. "I do appreciate it, dear. Really, I do. But I'm not ready to leave yet."

"As you wish. Take care, Irene."

The next on Janeway's extensive list of people to contact, rouse to action, or annoy sufficiently to assist her was "Red" Grady. He smiled when he saw her, but his eyes were sad. He didn't look like he was getting enough sleep.

"We've got to stop meeting like this," he joked.

She smiled without much enthusiasm. "Hello, Red. I don't suppose you've been able to get anywhere with Montgomery."

"It's like talking to a stone wall," Grady acknowledged.

"You should have been chosen to lead the project," she said sincerely, "and God knows I wish you had."

He shrugged. "It's an old and honored tradition for war heroes to be promoted to important offices, whether or not they're suited to it. At least he's not Grant." For a brief moment, his impish grin made his face glow; then it faded. "He's dug his heels in and it's now getting to be a matter of pride to him."

"The lives of three people hinge on a man's pride?" Janeway said, outraged.

"I'm sorry, Kathryn, but he feels they're a security risk, and he outranks me. At least they've got a good doctor looking out for them."

"They're lucky to have Kaz," Janeway agreed. "But they need to be released."

Grady sighed. "I'll keep trying, but if I push too hard he'll stop listening to me altogether. And Kathryn—this is going to get worse before it gets better."

When Libby returned to her cottage much, much later, she still hadn't slept a great deal. But she was feeling refreshed, calmer and more centered.

Harry would never have made it as a covert agent. His face was too open, too honest, and while he would never deliberately reveal in words the secret with which he had been entrusted, every plane of his body cried out that he carried the burden. His sweet face was shadowed, his body taut and tense. Libby wished she could tell him that she knew where he had been, what he had undergone, and, most likely, exactly what information he harbored, but she couldn't.

So she had held him through the night, and they had spoken in soft voices about things that had nothing to do with holograms, Borg, or *Voyager.*

She took a shower and reluctantly turned her mind back to gnawing at the problem. Covington wasn't a fool, however prickly around the edges she might be. Libby mentally started reviewing what she knew.

One: There was a mole leaking information and technology to the Orion Syndicate. Two: It would have to be someone placed sufficiently high enough to have access to that information. Three: The juiciest bit of technology around today was *Voyager.* Four: Montgomery, who was on the initial list of suspects, had suddenly been given access to *Voyager.* And not only that, but because of his position as head of Project Full Circle, the HoloStrike and the Borg infestation now had also come under his command.

But where was the evidence? Not only was Libby coming up dry with evidence that could point directly to Montgomery, but all the evidence Covington had provided to her was falling apart.

Suddenly, Libby's mind flashed back to the conversation she had been permitted to overhear between Covington and Montgomery. There was someone Covington had working for her that Montgomery wanted on his "team."

Wanted *back* on his team.

One of the first tenets she had learned about espionage was to follow the trail, even if it seemed to double back on itself. Current information was yielding nothing useful. The trail had grown cold, so Libby had to pick it up where it was still warm. If this scientist Trevor Blake had worked with Montgomery, he might be worth finding.

Libby felt a rush of excited calm settle over her. This was what she was good at. She wasn't trained as an expert to access computers, or dismantle weapons, or break codes. Her strength was in analyzing people and being so harmless in the process that they let their guard down.

Libby stepped out of the shower and looked at herself in the mirror. She'd been blessed with physical beauty, and while she wasn't arrogant, she was aware of how attractive she was. Her natural personality was open and friendly, and women didn't see her as competition because they quickly warmed up to her. Men liked to look at her. It was a reality she had learned to deal with long ago, and one she had turned to her advantage. To the Federation's advantage.

She'd find this Blake fellow, talk to him, and see what she could pry out of him. Perhaps he could give her the one thing she needed in order to make Montgomery a real suspect, someone charges would stick to, instead of just a slippery phantom.

Chapter
20

ADMIRAL KATHRYN JANEWAY HAD HAD ENOUGH.

She'd spent enough time hounding poor Red Grady and others. He was trying, but he couldn't do anything. And Montgomery was a lost cause by now. It was time to look elsewhere. Seated in her small living room was everyone from her old senior staff she'd been able to get in touch with: Chakotay, Tuvok, Kim, and Paris. Torres was away on Boreth, Tom had told her, and of course Seven and the Doctor still languished in a Starfleet prison cell. She looked around at the dear, familiar faces and hope filled her once again.

"We all know what's happening," she said. "We know about the virus, and we know they're covering it up. We know that Starfleet, indeed the Federation, somehow think that this outbreak is being directed or caused by either Seven and Icheb or perhaps *Voyager*'s own technology. They're blaming us instead of coming to us for help. We know that there's a holographic uprising that has resulted in several deaths, intentional or not, and that the Federation is now being forced to respond. Dr. Kaz dropped an oblique warning about the Doctor, and the thought that they might make some sort of example of him had occurred to me as well."

Her voice grew hard. "We know these things, but we're not allowed to do a damn thing about them. We can't discuss the virus with the innocent, unaware population of the Federation for fear of causing widespread panic. We can't help our own Doctor, who ought to be assisting Starfleet instead of being their prisoner. Seven and Icheb look worse each time I see them, and our pleas to allow them a regeneration chamber are being ignored. I for one am not about to sit here and watch my friends suffer, or remain still while my homeworld is about to be overrun with Borg."

"Admiral," Tuvok interjected. "You spent seven years abiding by Starfleet rules and regulations when you might easily have ignored them. Now that we have returned to the place where they can be enforced—"

"If they're denying Seven and Icheb access to something that is necessary to their health, then they've crossed the line into torture. And the Doctor hasn't even been officially charged with anything. They need him. If anyone can come up with a vaccine or a cure for this Borg virus, it's he. I'm not advocating breaking the law. At least," she amended, her blue eyes bright, "not yet."

She looked at them, each in turn. "Starfleet and the

Federation should be embracing us and our knowledge, not pushing us away. The people who could help the most in halting this dreadful virus are locked up, not in labs where they could assist. Seven of Nine has proved that she doesn't want to return to the collective. She's had the chance and refused it repeatedly. She could give Starfleet more information about the Borg in a minute than they could cobble together in years. But they're afraid of her."

She gave full rein to the anger, the sense of insult and injustice that raged through her. "I'm not going to let their fear, their ignorance, doom us. Here's what I propose."

They remained silent, attentive, while she outlined every aspect of her plan. When she had finished, no one spoke for a while.

"Anyone who wishes to may leave now, and I won't think the less of you. I know what I'm asking you to do. It could cost us our lives or at the very least, our careers, and I understand this."

No one moved.

"So it's agreed." She let herself smile. "I had hoped you'd all share my goals. I shouldn't have even doubted any of you."

She turned to her console and said, "Computer, open a channel to Captain Jean-Luc Picard on the *Enterprise*."

When Picard's distinguished mien appeared, Janeway saw at once that he was troubled. She wondered if he had been informed about the Borg outbreak, but since she wasn't sure, she said nothing. His somber face lightened only a little when he saw her.

"Admiral Janeway," he said. "An unexpected pleasure. What can I do for you?"

"I need to ask a favor, Captain," said Janeway. "I'm in an awkward situation. I have a friend who's in trouble. You have a crew member whose help would be invaluable. Would you be willing to lend him to us for a while?"

"Of whom are we speaking?"

Janeway told him.

It was a long few days for Jarem Kaz, with over a hundred and fifty patients to see. His exasperation with the situation grew with each patient that he examined and declared fit to be released. Why were they wasting his time? There was no evidence that any of *Voyager*'s crew had been even partially assimilated. No dormant nanoprobes, no unusual temperature changes, no erratic behavior, nothing.

Even Seven of Nine and Icheb, the most logical suspects, showed no signs of suddenly speaking in the plural or threatening people by declaring resistance was futile. He was troubled by the buzzing both former Borg reported experiencing in their implants, but it was obvious to anyone with first-year medical training that neither of them was in danger of losing her or his identity.

He had agreed wholeheartedly with bringing Seven and Icheb in for examination when the virus first reared its ugly head, but he saw no reason to keep them imprisoned any longer, except perhaps for their own safety. His heart broke for young Icheb, who was clearly devastated by the attack. As well he ought to be.

Kaz knew he was wasting his time here. He should be working with the other teams, helping to develop some kind of cure for this virus. He had access to the knowledge of nine different people, thanks to the Kaz symbiont, and the medical knowledge of the unjoined man he had once been.

And the Doctor! Why they didn't bring him in for consultation was beyond Kaz. Certainly he was a suspect in the HoloStrike and more serious recent set of attacks, but Kaz felt in his heart that the Doctor was involved only in the most peripheral sense, if indeed he was involved at all. He'd viewed many of the Doctor's logs and witnessed the evolution from an arrogant yet complex computer program into a compassionate . . . well . . . *person*. There was nothing in the Doctor's past history to make anyone believe he'd condone violence. And even if he was wrapped up in the issue of holographic rights, a planet full of Borg wouldn't serve the movement any at all. The Doctor had personal experience with the Borg. He could have helped. Hell, he could have helped a lot.

When Seven of Nine came in for her daily examination, he couldn't even summon up a reassuring smile for her, so deeply was he buried in his own black thoughts.

She looked awful, even worse than Icheb. She was pale and losing weight. She trembled slightly, and accepted his assistance when he reached to steady her as she climbed atop the diagonostic bed.

"I'm so sorry," he said. "I wish they'd let you two regenerate. I'll keep asking them, I assure you."

She gave him a fleeting smile. "Persistence is futile," she said, and despite the grim situation he chuckled.

More seriously, she said, "If I were indeed linked to the collective, my contact with them would only be strengthened during my regeneration period. Starfleet has documentation that it is during such times that the queen has been able to enter my thoughts. They would be foolish indeed not to take precautions."

"Don't get me started on this," he said. "You're *not* involved and I can prove it to them. These ridiculous 'precautions' are starting to hurt you. I can minimize the effects, but I can't stave them off forever." He looked at her with worried blue eyes. "Continued lack of regeneration could kill you both."

"I am aware of that."

"I wish I could get them to be." He pressed a hypo to her neck. It hissed gently, and her trembling stopped. But she was still unnaturally pale.

"Thank you, Doctor." Steadier than she was when she entered, this time she declined assistance. She strode out of sickbay with her fair head held high.

Kaz watched her go, troubled by her suffering, then glanced at the chronometer. There were over forty more people to be examined, but they would have to wait. It was time for the daily briefing, something Kaz dreaded more and more with each passing day.

The memories of the poet that belonged to the symbiont inside him stirred with beautiful, aching words as he regarded the haggard faces of his colleagues as they filed into the briefing room, taking chairs in silence. The air crackled with tension, but no one spoke, no one grabbed a cup of coffee, nothing. Montgomery stood at the head of the room, his weathered face looking even grimmer than usual, the lines on his face deeper than Kaz had seen them before.

"Everyone knows about the attacks of last week," he said without preamble. "Baines claims full responsibility for them, which makes our job a bit easier. We're going to have to take some steps. He complained that we didn't react sufficiently to his little HoloStrike. Well, by God, we're going to react now. I've put forth a request to have the program of every hologram on the level of the EMH Mark One altered. If we remove any knowledge of its situation, anything at all that prevents it from doing the menial jobs we want it to do, then we remove any interest in, desire for, or even comprehension of freedom. There's no need for the Mark Ones to know about microsurgery, or opera, or anything other than how to scrub conduits and mine dilithium. It's my understanding that this type of modification would be a simple task."

While everyone else around him was nodding approval, Kaz stared in horror. When the words exploded, it took him a second to realize that he was the one who was uttering them.

"You're talking the equivalent of a lobotomy for these programs!" he cried.

Montgomery fixed him with his fierce gaze. "You bet," he said. "That's exactly right. Keep them stupid and docile. Should have done that in the first place. I don't know why their programmers kept that kind of programming intact at all once they reassigned them."

"Will—will this affect *Voyager*'s Doctor?"

"He'll be the first one we do," Montgomery said. "We'll make an example of him."

"You can't do that! He has knowledge of the Borg that could help us cure this virus!"

Montgomery heaved an exaggerated sigh and folded his arms across his broad chest.

"You know, Dr. Kaz, I'm getting mighty tired of you telling me what I can and cannot do. Your position is a coveted one. You do your job well, but one more outburst like this one and you will be reassigned. Do we understand one another?"

Kaz swallowed. "Yes, sir," he said, the words almost choking him.

"Good. Knowing how slowly the wheels turn, it will take some time before I get approval to proceed, more's the pity. But at least we can start letting the public, and more importantly that bastard Baines, know what we're planning." He squared his shoulders. "And now to something a bit less pleasant."

He turned and touched some controls on the wall. A large holographic image of a globe appeared, hovering in the air above the twenty or so people assembled. Everyone craned their necks to look up at it.

"We've finally been able to get some estimates on what we're up against. We had an original outbreak of seven. Four children, two adults past the age of ninety, and one man suffering from Iverson's disease."

Seven small red dots appeared on various places around the globe—four in the northern hemisphere, three in the southern. There was no discernable geographic link.

"Within two weeks, it had risen to twenty-three."

The dots spread across the holographic representation of the Earth, some manifesting hundreds of kilometers away from the original outbreak sites, others clearly occurring because of direct contact. A few of the adult Borg that were appearing were capable of assimilation.

"It's now up to forty-six cases. Some have occurred within families, others are fresh, new outbreaks. We've got no knowledge of how it's spread, other than the usual manner of assimilation through forced insertion of nanoprobes, and that only accounts for about ten percent of the cases. The rest just seem to appear out of nowhere. Let me reemphasize this—only ten percent are Borg created through traditional means. The other ninety percent seem to be spontaneously becoming Borg for no reason we can yet understand."

"Is it still affecting only those with weak immune systems?" someone asked.

Montgomery glanced over at Kaz. "Care to field that one, Doctor?"

Kaz cleared his throat. "Thus far, yes. However, I've cross-referenced the virulence of the spread with that of other infectious diseases. By my calculation, it's only a matter of time, perhaps just a few days, until healthy adults start manifesting symptoms."

"And when that happens," said Montgomery, "we're looking at this."

As if the representation of the Earth were a living creature that had suddenly been pricked with thousands of holes, red began to bleed across its landmasses. Even though he'd been the one to help design this simulation. Kaz felt his stomach clench.

Mercilessly the red tide spread, blossoming like a deadly flower, until all but a few infinitesimal, isolated patches of land remained unconquered.

The Earth was covered with red.

Was covered with Borg.

Look for STAR TREK fiction from Pocket Books

Star Trek®

Star Trek: Voyager®

Enterprise®

Star Trek®: New Frontier

New Frontier #1-4 Collector's Edition • Peter David
    #1 • *House of Cards*
    #2 • *Into the Void*
    #3 • *The Two-Front War*
    #4 • *End Game*
#5 • *Martyr* • Peter David
#6 • *Fire on High* • Peter David
The Captain's Table #5 • *Once Burned* • Peter David
Double Helix #5 • *Double or Nothing* • Peter David
#7 • *The Quiet Place* • Peter David
#8 • *Dark Allies* • Peter David
#9-11 • *Excalibur* • Peter David
    #9 • *Requiem*
    #10 • *Renaissance*
    #11 • *Restoration*
Gateways #6: *Cold Wars* • Peter David
Gateways #7: *What Lay Beyond:* "Death After Life" • Peter David
#12 • *Being Human* • Peter David

Star Trek®: Stargazer

The Valiant • Michael Jan Friedman
Double Helix #6: *The First Virtue* • Michael Jan Friedman and Christie Golden
Gauntlet • Michael Jan Friedman
Progenitor • Michael Jan Friedman

Star Trek®: Starfleet Corps of Engineers (eBooks)

Have Tech, Will Travel (paperback) • various
    #1 • *The Belly of the Beast* • Dean Wesley Smith
    #2 • *Fatal Error* • Keith R.A. DeCandido
    #3 • *Hard Crash* • Christie Golden
    #4 • *Interphase, Book One* • Dayton Ward & Kevin Dilmore
Miracle Workers (paperback) • various
    #5 • *Interphase, Book Two* • Dayton Ward & Kevin Dilmore
    #6 • *Cold Fusion* • Keith R.A. DeCandido
    #7 • *Invincible, Book One* • Keith R.A. DeCandido & David Mack
    #8 • *Invincible, Book Two* • Keith R.A. DeCandido & David Mack
Some Assembly Required (paperback) • various
    #9 • *The Riddled Post* • Aaron Rosenberg
    #10 • *Gateways Epilogue: Here There Be Monsters* • Keith R.A. DeCandido
    #11 • *Ambush* • Dave Galanter & Greg Brodeur
    #12 • *Some Assembly Required* • Scott Ciencin & Dan Jolley
No Surrender (paperback) • various

Star Trek®: Section 31™

Rogue • Andy Mangels & Michael A. Martin
Shadow • Dean Wesley Smith & Kristine Kathryn Rusch
Cloak • S.D. Perry
Abyss • Dean Weddle & Jeffrey Lang

Star Trek®: Gateways

#1 • *One Small Step* • Susan Wright
#2 • *Chainmail* • Diane Carey
#3 • *Doors Into Chaos* • Robert Greenberger
#4 • *Demons of Air and Darkness* • Keith R.A. DeCandido
#5 • *No Man's Land* • Christie Golden
#6 • *Cold Wars* • Peter David
#7 • *What Lay Beyond* • various
Epilogue: Here There Be Monsters • Keith R.A. DeCandido

Star Trek® Omnibus Editions

Invasion! Omnibus • various
Day of Honor Omnibus • various
The Captain's Table Omnibus • various
Double Helix Omnibus • various
Star Trek: Odyssey • William Shatner with Judith and Garfield Reeves-Stevens
Millennium Omnibus • Judith and Garfield Reeves-Stevens
Starfleet: Year One • Michael Jan Friedman

Star Trek® Short Story Anthologies

Strange New Worlds, vol. I, II, III, IV, V, and VI • Dean Wesley Smith, ed.
The Lives of Dax • Marco Palmieri, ed.
Enterprise Logs • Carol Greenburg, ed.
The Amazing Stories • various

Other Star Trek® Fiction

Legends of the Ferengi • Ira Steven Behr & Robert Hewitt Wolfe
Adventures in Time and Space • Mary P. Taylor, ed.
Captain Proton: Defender of the Earth • D.W. "Prof" Smith
New Worlds, New Civilizations • Michael Jan Friedman
The Badlands, Books One and *Two* • Susan Wright
The Klingon Hamlet • Wil'yam Shex'pir
Dark Passions, Books One and *Two* • Susan Wright
The Brave and the Bold, Books One and *Two* • Keith R.A. DeCandido

STAR TREK®

STARGAZER: THREE

MICHAEL JAN FRIEDMAN

When a transporter mishap deposits a beautiful woman from another universe on the *Stargazer*, Gerda Asmond suspects the alien of treachery.

But she has to wonder—is she following her Klingon instincts or succumbing to simple jealousy?

Gerda needs to find out—or Picard and his crew may pay for their generosity with their lives.

Available August 2003

STST

STAR TREK®

STARGAZER: OBLIVION

MICHAEL JAN FRIEDMAN

In 1893, a time-traveling Jean-Luc Picard encountered a long-lived alien named Guinan, who was posing as a human to learn Earth's customs.

This is the story of a Guinan very different from the woman we think we know.

A Guinan who yearns for oblivion.

Available September 2003